Americans in Paris

Americans in Paris

GREAT SHORT STORIES OF THE CITY OF LIGHT

SELECTED BY
STEVEN GILBAR

Foreword by
Diane Johnson

CAPRA PRESS
SANTA BARBARA
PUBLISHER OF MEMORABLE BOOKS SINCE 1969

Copyright ©Steven Gilbar
All rights reserved
Printed in the United States of America

Published by Capra Press
815 De La Vina Street
Santa Barbara, CA 93101
www.caprapress.com

Cover and book design by Lucy Brown Design
"Paris Bicycle," photo by Peter Treadwell
Body type is Adobe Garamond

Library of Congress Cataloging-in-Publication Data
Americans in Paris: Great Short Stories in the City of Light
Selected by Steven Gilbar
p. cm.

ISBN 0-9722503-0-1 (trade paperback)

Library of Congress Control Number: 2002109971

*To Janice & Peter
and Annie & Gary
who love Paris*

Books edited by Steven Gilbar:

The Book Book

Good Books: A Book Lover's Companion

The Open Door: When Writers First Learned to Read

Tales of Santa Barbara

Red Tiles, Blue Skies: More Tales of Santa Barbara

The Reader's Quotation Book: A Literary Companion

Reading in Bed: Personal Essays on the Glories of Reading

Natural State: A Literary Anthology of California Nature Writing

Literary Santa Barbara

Santa Barbara Stories

California Shorts

L.A. Shorts

L.A. Noir

Published & Perished: Memoria, Eulogies & Remembrances of American Writers

Contents

FOREWARD BY DIANE JOHNSON   17

INTRODUCTION BY STEVEN GILBAR   21

ALICE ADAMS
    Winter Rain   27

HORTENSE CALISHER
    Il Plœ:r Dā Mō Kœ:r   41

EVAN S. CONNELL
    Madame Broulard   51

JOAN FRANK
    The Waiting Room   63

ELLEN GILCHRIST
    Paris   79

MARK HELPRIN
    Lightning North of Paris   97

JAMES LAUGHLIN
    The River   105

ROBERT McALMON
    The Highly Prized Pajamas   123

STEPHEN MINOT
    A Death in Paris   139

WAVERLY ROOT
    Carmencita   157

DANIEL STERN
    The #63 Bus from the Gare De Lyon   167

PETER TAYLOR
    Je Suis Perdu   175

PAUL THEROUX
    Portrait of a Lady   193

LILY TUCK
    Rue Guynemer   207

Was it fun in Paris? Who did you see there and was the Madeleine pink at five o'clock and did the fountains fall with hollow delicacy into the framing of space in the Place de la Concorde, and did the blue creep out from behind the Colonades of the rue de Rivoli through the grille of the Tuileries and was the Louvre gray and metallic in the sun and did the trees hang brooding over the cafés and were there lights at night and the click of saucers and the auto horns that play Debussey—
  I love Paris. How was it?

–Zelda Fitzgerald
(from a letter to her daughter)

Foreword

The narrator of Peter Taylor's story "Je Suis Perdu" apologizes diffidently for writing about his love for Paris:
"Nothing could be so anticlimactic as an American living on the left bank of the Seine and taking a morning walk in the Jardins du Luxembourg. He remembered two novels whose first chapters took for their setting this very spot. Nothing was so deadening to a place as literature!"

Luckily the reverse is not true. There is nothing so enlivening to literature as an account of beloved places, as we see in this wonderful collection of Americans-in-Paris stories by 20th-century American writers.

The romance of American writers and Paris goes back much farther than Hemingway and James Baldwin, F. Scott Fitzgerald and James Jones. Those legendary writer-travelers of our recent past—Henry James and Edith Wharton a hundred years ago, Benjamin Franklin, Thomas Jefferson and Tom Paine a hundred years before that—were also Paris-lovers, and this attraction of American writers to Paris continues to our day. What is striking is the similarity of the American experience over the more than two centuries.

The experience of the American in Paris goes beyond mere tourism to an essential aspect of our growth. Almost without exception in these stories, the writer comes to Paris to find something, usually expressed as "himself" or "herself," and either does or doesn't, or loses something and goes home. These writers all return to become famous American writers, in fact, but not without trying to examine what it was they gained or lost. "She had come to France for a change of scene and to learn the language," Lily Tuck writes of her heroine. Maybe that is all there is to it on the surface, but there is more, much more.

A wish to celebrate the beauty of Paris emerges in all these stories, suggesting an aesthetic dimension that is for all of us an important part of our experience of Paris. Each writer shows the same love of evoking the places familiar to all of us from other stories: from films, books, or our own wanderings, from the Jardins du Luxembourg to the Deux Magots to the cemetery of Pére Lachaise. But three more important subjects, perhaps, are sex, wine, and ideas of comportment—subjects that characters in most Paris stories find themselves involved with, things America did not, at least until recently, furnish with the same lack of reservation.

Americans go to Paris with the determined sense that there are things they ought to know—and aren't going to find them out by staying home. But even the heady excitement of doing things in France in relative safety that couldn't or wouldn't be done at home does not quite supply the answer to what the mysterious gift is that Paris gives or, more often, judging from these stories, mysteriously withholds, as it withholds from the hero of Paul Theroux's "Portrait of a Lady" when he leaves "feeling insulted and had never hated himself more," faced with the lack within himself.

His is not the only defeat. When the narrator of James Laughlin's "The River," about the adventures of two boys from Springfield, Illinois, writes, "I came to have, to really have and really know, what we had tried so hard to find and never found. I came to be a writer and began to be a man," we somehow don't believe him. He's back in Springfield, the lessons learned, if any, unarticulated.

The couple in Daniel Stern's story decide to literally plant themselves back in the USA by buying a cemetery plot there. As literature in general concerns adaptation to reality, if not by resignation then by death, and Paris represents the ideal against which mere reality, in our case America, will always be tested, a taste of Paris is never without the special bittersweet flavor of writers looking back and glimpsing something of the elusive thing they sought that was forever a little out of reach.

If the writer of a preface may be permitted some words of personal reminiscence, it happens I have met most of the writers whose stories make up this delightful volume. As writers and people, they are not at all alike, but there are the certain recurrent themes I have mentioned in all the stories. "Winter Rain," by the late Alice Adams, a beloved friend and fellow San Franciscan, was already a favorite of mine and describes a year in the late forties about which Alice often also spoke. The meaning to her of her year in Paris, so brilliantly evoked in "Winter Rain," was summarized even more succinctly when she would say that Paris was where she was constantly falling back on her most perfected phrase from French class: "Je n'ai acune idee," I have no idea. Having no idea is a particularly American privilege in Paris—the French themselves are, and are supposed to be, instructed and knowing, above all in the ways of their own culture.

The American experience there is, in a way, so unchanging it is hard to realize that these stories take place over several decades, beginning in the late twenties. If Americans don't change and the city itself doesn't change—Robert McAlmon's Paris is only a little different from Ellen Gilchrist's—it is worth noting how much the French themselves have changed, from the proud but penurious post-war society, with its terrible economies and chilly rooms so vividly evoked in Adams's story (and in a number of the others) to the rich, comfortable nation of today.

One senses the French to be more themselves now than they were just after the war, but we Americans are as much as ever searching for ourselves, seeking some level of civilization that constantly eludes us.

Introduction

If you love Paris in the springtime (or any time,) you will love these short stories which richly evoke the mood of the City of Light. They, of course, are not *about* Paris; they are about human situations played out in Paris where the city is palpably felt. The principal characters are all Americans; some are students, scholars, or expatriates, Others are on missions, on business, on vacation. They wander a Paris occupied by bistros and boites, clubs and cafés, trying to puzzle out its mysteries.

American writers have been drawn to Paris since the mid-19th century, a long line that includes Henry James and Edith Wharton, Ernest Hemingway and Gertrude Stein, Henry Miller and Anais Nin, through Adam Gopnik and David Sedaris. Paris has worked its magic on them as it has on so many other Americans. Many have written novels about Americans in Paris—from Henry James' *Portrait of a Lady* to James Baldwin's *Giovanni's Room* right up to Diane Johnson's *La Mariage*. Often they have aided readers in creating a Paris of the mind, a city that would be later reified by an actual journey, actual adventures. In this collection you will meet other Americans who had their own particular adventures in Paris.

After World War II many American writers drifted over to Paris where they could write and live cheaply. Among them was the novelist and short-story writer Alice Adams (1926-1999) She and her then-husband stayed in a hotel called Le Welcome on the rue de Seine in the neighborhood around the Café de Flore and the Deux-Magots and the church St Germain-des-Prés. She later wrote that "we knew almost everyone we saw on the streets, or at least we knew who they were. I remember standing there on the boulevard one day when someone pointed across to a man coming out of the Brasserie Lipp, saying, 'Look, there's Picasso!' and it was, those incredible eyes unmistakable, even at that distance." That special time and place is richly evoked in "Winter Rain."

In "Il Plœ:r Dā Mō Kœ:r" Hortense Calisher, a three-time winner of the O. Henry prize for the short story, gives fictional gloss to her own 1950's misadventure in the hazards of using schoolbook French in France.

Around the same time Evan S. Connell was living in Paris, where he fell in with a crowd of young American expatriates, most of them trying their hands at writing, painting, sculpture, or music. Among them, George Plimpton was to become one of the more important, in large part, because he started, with a couple of friends, *The Paris Review*, which in the first few years of its publishing life featured early short stories by little-known writers such as Philip Roth, Terry Southern, Samuel Beckett—and Evan S. Connell. However, the café society of his fellow expatriates did not hold much attraction for Connell and by 1955 he was back in the United States, living in San Francisco. Those Paris years are imaginatively recreated in his characteristic concise style in "Madame Broulard."

The next three stories are about love and its variations. Joan Frank's "The Waiting Room" tells the story of a lonely American woman searching for love. Ellen Gilchrist, the National Book Award-winning writer who spent most of her childhood in Issaquena County, Mississippi, not surprisingly, has set most of her fiction in the South. But not always: In "Paris" her recurrent heroine, Rhoda Manning, finds herself in one of the author's favorite cities. Mark Helprin began publishing short stories in *The New Yorker* shortly after graduating from Harvard in the late sixties. His 1981 collection *Ellis Island and Other Stories* was nominated for the National Book Award. In "Lightning North of Paris" a young composer struggling with love and his art in Paris imbued with "magical realism."

The two stories that follow go back a couple of decades. James Laughlin (1914-1997), best known as the founder of New Directions, the foremost American publisher of avant-garde writers of the twentieth century, was also a poet, essayist, and writer of elegantly crafted short stories. "The River" written in the late 1930s, when the author was living in Paris, captures the excitement of the young artist trying to find his way in the city.

"The Highly Prized Pajamas," was written by Robert McAlmon (1895-1956), an American writer and proprietor of Contact Editions, a Paris imprint that published expatriate writers. His take on the "Lost Generation" in Paris during the 1920s, perhaps the most exhilarating decade in the history of modern literature, can be found in his 1938 memoir, *Being Geniuses Together*. Once described as an "ambisexual dilettante" and as "sardonic" he liked to haunt the demimonde world of the Latin Quarter, where he sets the cynical, stylistic tale presented here about a prostitute (*poule*) who prowled it and an American caught in her web.

Novelist and short-story writer Stephen Minot, a self described francophile, tries to spend time in Paris whenever he can. "A Death in Paris" is an interesting tale of the demise of an American expat.

Waverley Root (1903-1982), best known for his erudite and charming books about French and Italian cuisine, was the editor of the Paris edition of the *Chicago Tribune* in the early 1930s. "Carmencita" drolly captures that time and the antics of the young American reporters living the fast life.

Married couples are at the center of the next two stories. In "The #63 Bus from the Gare de Lyon," Daniel Stern, author of nine novels and four story collections, tells a story of an American couple vacationing in Paris and reminds us of the fragility and sweetness of life. The Tennessee-born writer, Peter Taylor (1917-1994), winner of the Pulitzer Prize for his novel *A Summons to Memphis*, spent a year with his wife and two children during the 1950s in France on a Fulbright Grant. His subtle, carefully crafted short stories often deal with family life, as does "Je Suis Perdu" about an American writer, his wife and two children, about to leave Paris after a year's stay there.

Paul Theroux, novelist, short story writer, and author of several best-selling travel books, lived for many years in London during the 1970s and 80s. Many of his stories deal with outsiders who attempt to come to terms with an alien culture. His story here, "Portrait of a Lady," with its allusion to the novel of Henry James of the same name, does not reflect the latter's regard for an old culture: his American innocent abroad is no Francophile.

The collection concludes with a story by Lily Tuck, who was born in Paris and spoke French before learning English. She has lived a cosmopolitan life and now divides her time between Maine and New York City. Her affection for her native city is apparent in her elegant and enigmatic story of one Parisian street, "Rue Guynemer."

Reading these stories may take you back to the Paris you fell in love with, but may also show you another Paris where you will walk the Left Bank, eat in a brasserie, saunter through Les Halle, and watch the children play at the Luxembourg Gardens. They, like Proust's madelaine, may send you off on a journey to the most wonderful of cities. Bon Voyage!

Winter Rain

ALICE ADAMS

Whenever in the final unendurable weeks of winter, I am stricken, as now, to the bone with cold—it is raining, the furnace has somehow failed—I remember that winter of 1947–1948 in Paris, when I was colder than ever in my life, when it always rained, when everything broke down. That was the winter of strikes: GRÈVE GÉNÉRALE, in large strange headlines. And everyone struck: Métro, garbage, water, electricity, mail—all these daily necessities were at one time or another with difficulty forgone. Also, that was the first winter of American students—boys on the G.I. bill and girls with money from home, Bennington meeting Princeton in the Montana Bar. There were cellar clubs to which French friends guided one mysteriously: on the Rue Dauphine the Tabu, with a band; the Mephisto, just off the Boulevard Saint-Germain; and further out on Rue Blomet the wicked Bal Nègre, where one danced all night to West Indian music, danced with everyone and drank Pernod. It was a crowded, wild, excited year.

I think of friends of that time—I have kept up with none of them, certainly not with Bruno, nor Laura, nor Joe, not even with Mme. Frenaye. And it gloomily occurs to me that they may all be dead, Bruno in some violent Italian way, Laura and Joe in Hollywood, and Mme. Frenaye of sheer old age, on the Rue de Courcelles, "tout près," as she used to say, "du Parc Monceau." Though we parted less than friends, it is she of whom I think most often.

Madame and I really parted, as from the first I should have known we would, over money. And, more than I regret the loss of our connection, I regret the sordidness of its demise. But I should have known; the process was gradual but clear. As was the fact that I, and not she, would lose face in any conflict.

To begin with, she extracted from me an enormous amount of money for permission to live at the cold end of the long drafty hall in her flat. Of course I didn't have to take the room, or to accept the arrangement at all, but from the first I was seduced. I had heard, from friends, that a Mme. Frenaye might be willing to take a nice American girl student into her charming home. I inquired further, and was invited to tea. It was raining dreadfully, even in September, and I wore, all wet and shivering, a yellow summer coat and summer dress since, probably owing to a strike somewhere, my trunk of winter clothes had not arrived. The street seemed impossibly gray, chilled and forbidding, but the central room of the flat into which I was ushered by Madame was warm and graceful. There were exquisite white Louis XVI chairs, a marvelous muted blue Persian rug, a mantel lined with marble above a fireplace in which a small fire blazed prettily.

Mme. Frenaye was a great goddess of a woman. She must have been sixty, or even seventy—I was never sure—but she was very tall and she held herself high; she was Junoesque indeed. She still mourned her husband, dead five years, and wore only black, but her effect was vivid. Her hair was bright gold and she wore it in a thick crowning braid across the waves that rose from her brow. Her eyes were very blue, capable of a great spectacle of innocence or charming guile, and she wore mascara heavily on her long lashes. She had dimples and perfect white teeth.

We took tea from a beautiful table before the fire, and we talked about Antibes where I had spent the summer. Mme. Frenaye poured a little rum from a pretty porcelain jug into the tea, and said, "I would not have thought of going to the Riviera in the summer. So crowded then. But of course you are so young, you have not been to France before."

She seemed prepared to forgive, and I did not want to protest that I had had a very good time.

She went on, "But a winter in Paris, there you have chosen

wisely, this time you will not regret your choice. Theatre, opera, it is all here for you, the best in the world. And of course the Sorbonne, since you have chosen to study." She was vastly amused to learn the name of my course at the Sorbonne was Cours de la civilisation française. "But you will spend the rest of your life—" she said, and I agreed.

We talked and drank our tea, and ate small delicious cakes, until it occurred to me that I had perhaps stayed too long and so rose to leave. I think I had really forgotten that I had come about a room, or perhaps such a crass consideration seemed inappropriate in Louis XVI surroundings. Instead, on the way out I admired a painting. Mme. Frenaye said, "Ah, yes, and it has a gross value." I translate literally to give the precise effect of her words on me. My French was not good, and I thought I had misheard her, or not known an idiom. I would not be warned.

Then, at the door, while helping me with my still damp yellow coat, she said that she had heard that I needed a pleasant place to live, that she would be willing to let me live there, that she would serve me breakfast and dinner, and she named an outrageous number of francs. Even translated into dollars it was high. I was so stunned by her whole method that I accepted on the spot, and it was agreed that I would bring my things on the following Monday. That I did not even ask to see the room is evidence of my stupor; I must have thought it would be exactly like the salon.

And sometimes now I wonder whether she had any idea that I would accept; or made up that ridiculous figure simply to let me off. And I wonder too if I did not want to prove that I could do better than yellow coats and summer dresses in a cold September rain; behind me there were sound American dollars, and, as my father would have said, more where they came from. So, from our combined dubious motives, we were joined, to live and eat and talk together throughout those difficult historic months from September until February, until our private war became visible and manifest, and I left.

The room was actually not as bad as it might have been, taken on such dazzled faith. It was not large, nor warm, nor did it contain a desk or a bookcase; however, the bed was regally gilded and huge and soft, and I slept under comforting layers of down, between pink linen sheets. Madame sighed, her beautiful eyes misted as she showed the bed to me and I felt badly about so depriving her until I realized that her own small bed-sitting room had been astutely chosen as the warmest room in the house. And the grand bed would not fit into it.

When I said such things to Laura and Joe, later to Bruno, as we hunched over beers in the steamy Café de Flore or the Deux Magots, they reasonably exclaimed, "But why on earth do you stay there?" (Laura and Joe were Marxists, and I was acceptable to them partly because my arrangement with Mme. Frenaye left me with virtually no money at all.) In any case I did not think that they would feel the charm of Mme. Frenaye, and so I would say to them, "But the food is fantastic, and see how my French is improving."

Both of these things were quite true. I have never since tasted anything to compare with her poisson normand, that beautifully flaking fat white fish baked with tiny mushrooms, tiny shrimps and mussels in white wine. I have the most vivid sensual memories of her crisp green salads. I would arrive cold and usually wet from my long Métro trek, and hurriedly unwrap myself from my coat just in time to enter that small warm room where she had placed the white-clothed table. The room was full of marvelous delicate smells of hot food, and Madame in passage from the kitchen would greet me. "Bon soir, Patience. Mais vous avez froid. Asseyez-vous, je viens tout de suite. Oh, mais j'ai oublié l'essentiel—" and she was off to fetch the decanter of wine.

And my French did improve. She knew no English, and we talked animatedly throughout those months of dinners. She was endlessly curious about America, though she pretended to disbelieve half of what I told her. "But, Patience, surely you exaggerate," she would chide, in a tone of amused tolerance. Sometimes, fresh from Joe's lectures, I became heavily sociological. She listened intently, nodded appropriately. Only when I hit on American anti-Semitism did I strike some chord in her—she found it absolutely incomprehensible. She adored American Jews. Her husband had been a cotton merchant, and in his business the only Americans he met were Jewish or from Texas. And the Texans, according to Madame, were appalling: they ordered the most expensive champagne or cognac and then got drunk on it. The Jewish families whom she met were quite another story. "Tellement cultivées, tellement sensibles." Her most admired American friends, the Berkowitzes ("Ah, les Berkowitz"), went to museums daily, to the theatre and the opera; the Texans never. She felt that "les Berkowitz" too squandered their money but in less visible and offensive ways. One of her most loved stories was of going shopping for a brassiere, a soutien-gorge, with Marion Berkowitz. "C'était tout, tout petit," she would say, with her thumb and forefinger gesturing a pinch of nothing, "et ça coétait tellement cher!" This contradiction never ceased to amaze and delight her.

The truth was that I liked Mme. Frenaye. I admired her beauty and her charm; and her scorn, her assumption of superiority to the world, comforted me since I felt that she counted me on her side. Moreover, I simply could not imagine a scene in which I told her that I was going to leave. I think that if I had not met Bruno, near Christmas, during one long night in the Bal Nègre, where I had reluctantly gone with Laura and Joe, I would have lived on the Rue de Courcelles until June, when I took that huge and final boat for New York.

My memory of Bruno is also involved with the cold: I see the two of us clinging together in a garish white-lit Métro entrance because it was too cold outside, and our partings were endless and all unendurable. We walked together. I remember my ungloved hand pressing against his, together jammed deeply into his shabby tweed pocket, as we walked past steamed bright windows in the iron cold, stopping to kiss. Even Bruno seems legendary to me now; both our romantic intensity and the facts of his life sound mythic. His father was an Italian anti-Fascist who had left Italy in the Twenties. Bruno was born in Toulouse, and spent his fifteenth birthday in a Vichy concentration camp, his sixteenth in a similar camp in Italy. He had fought with the Maquis, and with guerrilla fighters in the Italian Alps. He had no scars nor any limp to show for all of this; he was tall and sturdy, smooth-skinned, clear-eyed as any innocent American boy—in fact he was often taken for a G.I., which amused him and privately annoyed me. He studied law in Paris, and lived with relatives out in the 14th arrondissement. Thus in the cold we had no place to go, and between partings we dreamed of a furnished room, warm and light, anywhere in Paris. I can no longer remember the substance of our quarrels, nor of our talk, but both went on forever, punctuating each other, and all the time our eyes held together, our hands touched. Out of some misguided sense of duty I spent Christmas Day that year with Madame rather than with Bruno. And it was a bad day. Madame was far from being at her best. She sniffed deprecatingly at my gift of a tiny bottle of perfume from Worth, telling me she had once calculated the contents of all the bottles on her dressing table and it came to more than two liters. "You can imagine," she said, "how much that would be worth." She had given me a pair of felt slippers from Trois Quartiers, and they were not very pretty.

We rallied somewhat at dinner. There was an incredible roast chicken, an unheard-of luxury in Paris that year. But then, with the token glass of brandy, Mme. Frenaye grew sad again, and spoke of the death of her husband. "Over and over he said to me, 'Ah, how good you are,'" and her great eyes misted. I was wildly impatient to go; I had promised to meet Bruno at the Flore at nine. I wanted to hear of no other love, no death.

That night we fought because I lived so far away. Bruno found incomprehensible my refusal to move. "On purpose you isolate yourself in your gray prison," he said. (Once he had accompanied me home, had seen from the outside the fortress of apartments on the Rue de Courcelles.) He said, his clear blue eyes near mine, "How much more time we would have if you even lived near the Sorbonne—I think you don't want to be with me—you would rather stay safely beside your little fire." I protested this violently, but in a sense it was perfectly true. I was afraid of him; life with Madame, though difficult, seemed safer than the exposure of a room alone.

But at the same time that I resisted Bruno I found my fortress more and more impossible. I was extremely tense; the most petty annoyances grew large. I once calculated that with all the small sums of money which Madame had borrowed from time to time to tip porters, buy stamps, I could have bought Bruno a gaudy present.

And there was the matter of my CARE packages. My anxious mother sent them punctually each month, thus assuring herself that I would never starve. I had written and asked her not to. Their arrival embarrassed me; I was sure the porter who carried them upstairs knew what they were, and thought of his own hungry family. I wanted badly to give them to him, but some misplaced shyness held me back. Madame adored all that American food. She appropriated each package and opened it on the marble-topped kitchen table. She exclaimed over, and later used, the boxes of cake mix, and she devised a marvelous method of stuffing baked potatoes with the liver paté that came in large cans. The pancake mix she especially loved. "Ah, les crêpes américaines," she would cry out lovingly, expressing her whole indulgent fondness for the young rich crazy country of dollars and handsome brave G.I.s, of fantastic machines that did everything, of her cherished Berkowitzes and of me.

But in my new mood of sullen resentment I protested her appropriation. How dare she charge me ruinous rates for food and lodging and then accept such a bulk of food from my mother? In silence and secrecy my list of grievances against her mounted; that they were petty and degrading of course made them more unbearable. Also that I lacked the courage to say anything.

It was perfectly appropriate to that year that my dilemma was finally resolved by a strike. And by Bruno.

All during January, Bruno snarled and complained at my living arrangements. I remember an afternoon in the upstairs part of the Flore, where it was always warm and with luck one could stay for hours, seated on the plaid-covered banquettes, without having to order anything. We had, I remember, not enough money between us for hot chocolate—which we both felt could have saved the afternoon. Unkindly, Bruno reminded me that if I lived in the Quarter, in a cheap room, I could now be making hot chocolate and serving it in privacy. There was always a sort of European practicality about him—even in love, I thought—and in the phrase betrayed how American was my own romanticism. He gave a sense of the pressure of time, of destiny, as though along his way he could not be troubled with incidents of geography and money. By the end of the afternoon we had agreed never to meet again, and I wept conspicuously all the long Métro ride from Odéon to Place Péreire.

The next week was unendurable. There was a violent cold black rain. The heat failed again in Madame's long flat, the fires spluttered and would not burn. Wholly miserable, I mourned my forever lost love.

Then came the mail strike. No letters at all, from anywhere. The papers described mountains of paper piled fantastically on post-office floors. I was completely dependent on letters from home for money, and now I could not pay Madame on the day when my fee came due. At dinner I tried to mention it casually to her. Much in the spirit of the times, I said, "After all, this strike can't go on forever."

But Madame's spirit was not at all with the times. "Strike or not, I have to shop for groceries," she said with uncharacteristic terseness. I was totally upset; life, I felt, was too much for me; I had no resources. And even Madame, stronger and wiser and infinitely more charming, fell down. Apropos of nothing she told me again the story of Marion Berkowitz and the buying of the soutien-gorge, but the mention of high prices made us both nervous and we failed to be amused.

That night, hunched frozen between the pink linen sheets, I decided that if I did not see Bruno again I would die.

At breakfast my final long-delayed scene with Mme. Frenaye took place, over cups of powdered American coffee from my latest CARE package. I found that I had to say everything all at once. "I have to move," I said. "It's very nice here but I simply can't afford it any longer. And really, you know, no one pays so much for a pension, I mean even in America this would be considered high. And also this is too far from my classes at the Sorbonne—you remember during the Métro strike I couldn't even get there."

Madame listened to this somewhat with the air of a teacher of speech. And indeed it was a tribute to the French I had learned with her that I was able to get it out. She seemed, on the whole, to approve both my eloquence and my logic, for at the end she said, "Certainement," in a final tone.

I needed her to argue with me, and I added defiantly, "I want to live in the Latin Quarter."

"Oui, le Quartier Latin." But she was not thinking about my proposed life on the Left Bank; her tone was completely neutral. And hearing it I realized suddenly that as far as she was concerned I had already gone. Also, and this was doubly infuriating, I realized that she had undoubtedly known for some time that I would go. Probably from that first wet day when we took our tea by her pretty fire she had known that I would not last the year. Any concession on her part—if she had said she could wait for the rent—might have made me weaken. But she was far too realistic and too economical for any emotional waste.

And so I packed that afternoon in a fury of frustration. I felt that I had been taken, conned out of my moment of righteous defiance by some ageless European trick of charm. As I hunted for shoe bags, I thought furiously that she had completely turned the tables. I was the one who had ended by being mercenary, petty. She came to the door later, and asked perfunctorily if there was anything that she could do to help, and I wanted to shout "No!" at her, but I did not; I only muttered negatively. She said, "Well, in that case I will say au revoir, Patience, et bonne chance."

We shook hands at the door to my erstwhile bedroom, and I said that I would call her when I was settled, and she said, "But please do," and smiled with her beautiful wise blue eyes and was gone. I had no true parting scene.

The room that I found late that afternoon was on the Rue de Seine. My high narrow windows overlooked the entrance to the Club Mephisto; I could see a fish market where the fat silver bellies were piled high, and a fruit stand bright with winter tomatoes and bunches of dark rose chrysanthemums. At the corner hardware store I bought a saucepan and a small tripod burner with some cans of Sterno, and felt myself prepared for warm domestic peace with Bruno.

But though reunited we were never peaceful. In spite of my room, of which he approved, our passionate partings continued. I can hear now the angry sound of his boots on the narrow steep stairs as he left stormily after an impossible argument. And I remember lying half awake dreaming that he would come back.

One afternoon, during a rift with Bruno that was more prolonged than usual, on an impulse I called Mme. Frenaye and asked her to have tea with me at the Ritz. She would be delighted, she said, and I remember that I wore my first New Look dress, which was gray silk with a terribly long skirt. The occasion was a great success. I was struck by how glad I was to see her. It seemed to me then that I had missed her, and that my life alone had been more difficult. Certainly that afternoon Madame was at her best. She complained pleasantly that the service was not what it had been before the war, nor the pastry, and after our tea we gossiped happily about the other women in the room.

Madame did not ask me about my present living arrangements. Since I had come prepared to boast this was slightly irritating, but at the same time I was relieved. Nor did she, as I had rather expected, say that she missed me. She was quite impersonally charming, and we parted with an exchange of pleasantries, but with no talk of a further meeting.

The rain and cold continued into April. I remember bitterly deciding that the lyric burst one expected of spring in Paris would never come, that it was a myth.

Joe and Laura had left, apologizing, for Hollywood in March. I went to lectures at the Sorbonne and in the lengthening intervals when I did not see Bruno I wandered alone about the city, hunched against the rain, wrapped in American tweed.

For at least a month Bruno and I got along happily. It was the tender penultimate stage of a love affair, before it became clear that I really wanted him to come to America and marry me, and that he wanted to live in Italy and did not want to get married, clear to us both that I was hopelessly domestic and bourgeois. He said, finally, that I would not be a suitable companion for an Italian statesman, and of course he was perfectly right.

But before this finality, in some spirit of bravado, I called Mme.

Frenaye and asked her to come to tea in my room—and asked Bruno to come too. I am not at all sure what I expected of either of them; perhaps I felt the dramatic necessity of a meeting between the two people who had that year been, variously, most important to me.

Or perhaps this was my last defiance of Madame. If that were so I failed utterly, foiled again by her aplomb. Of course Bruno helped; he appeared uncharacteristically in a white shirt and tie, his brown hair brushed smooth; he could not have looked less like an Italian radical with a violent past. Mme. Frenaye first took him to be a nice American boy; her whole demeanor spoke a total acceptance and approval of him. She thought it very wise of him to study law in Paris, and she raised her lovely innocent blue eyes in attractive horror when he told her how many hours he had to study each day. "But then you are so young and strong," she said, with a tender and admiring smile. Of course he liked her—who could not?

She even approved of my room, though she sat rather stiffly and gingerly on the single straight wooden chair. She looked across the street to the piles of fish and remarked that she had noticed lower prices here than in her own quartier, but this was her only suggestion that I had come down in the world. And I thought then, but did not speak, of her beautiful poisson normand. She only said, "Such a nice clean room, Patience, and it must be so convenient for you."

I made tea, boiling the water over Sterno which Madame thought terribly ingenious, and we ate the pastries which I had bought. Bruno and Madame talked about the beauties of Italy, of Florence in early spring, Venice in October. And painting. I could imagine her saying of him, "Tellement cultivé, ce jeune Italien, tellement sensible."

After that day everything deteriorated. The weather turned cold and it rained fiercely as though to remind us all of the difficult past winter. When, finally, I booked passage on a boat which was to leave the third of June, I felt that my exit was being forced, the city and the time would have no more of me. I had accepted the impossibility of Bruno—we still saw each other but I wept and it always ended badly. I did not see Madame again. I did call her, meaning to say good-bye, but there was no answer.

Sometimes it occurs to me to write to Madame, to send her pictures of my husband, my house and my children, as though to convince her that I have grown up, that I am no longer that odd girl who came to her in the wet summer coat, or who tried to charm her with tea made over Sterno in an unlikely room. Or I try to imagine her here, perhaps as the great-aunt whom, on shopping trips into town, I occasionally visit. But this is impossible: my aunt, an American Gothic puritan with a band of black grosgrain ribbon about her throat, my aunt laughing over the purchase of a tiny soutien-gorge, bringing in wine, l'essentiel? This won't do. And I am forced to leave Madame, and Bruno of whom I never think, as and where they are, in that year of my own history.

Il Plœːr Dã Mõ Kœːr

Hortense Calisher

I was taught to speak French with tears. It was not I who wept, or the other girls in my high-school class, but the poet Verlaine—the one who wrote "Il plœːr dã mō kœːr." Inside forty slack American mouths, he wept phonetically for almost a semester. During this time, we were not taught a word of French grammar or meaning—only the International Phonetic Alphabet, the sounds the symbols stood for, and Verlaine translated into them. We could not even pick up the celebrated pen of our aunt. But by the time Verlaine and our teacher Mlle. Girard had finished with us, we were indeed ready to pick it up, and in the most classically passionate accents this side of the Comédie Française.

Mlle. Girard achieved her feat in this way. On the very first morning, she explained to us that French could never be spoken properly by us Anglo-Saxons unless we learned to reanimate those muscles of the face, throat, *poitrine* that we possessed—even as the French—but did not use. Ours, she said, was a speech almost without lilt, spoken on a dead level of intonation, "like a sobway train."

"Like this," she said, letting her jaw loll idiotically and choosing the most American subject she could find: "Ay wahnt sahm ay-iss cream." French, on the other hand, was a language *passionné* and *spirituel*, of vowels struck without pedal, of "L's" made with a sprightly tongue tip—a sound altogether unlike our "l" which we made with our tongues plopping in our mouths. By her manner, she implied that all sorts of national differences might be assumed from this, although she could not take the time to pursue them.

She placed a wiry thumb and forefinger, gray with chalk dust, on either side of her mouth. "It is these muscles 'ere I shall teach you to use," she said. (If that early we had been trained to think in phonetic-symbols, we would have known that what she had actually said was "mœslz.") When she removed her hand, we saw that she had two little, active, wrinkling pouches, one on either side of her mouth. In the ensuing weeks I often wondered whether all French people had them, and we would get them, too. Perhaps only youthful body tone saved us, as, morning after morning, she went among us pinching and poking our lips into grimaces and compelling sudden ventriloquisms from our astonished sinuses.

As a final coup, she taught us the classic "r." "Demoiselles," she said, "this is an *élégance* almost impossible for Americans, but you are a special class—I think you may do it." By this time, I think she had almost convinced herself that she had effected somatic changes in our Anglo-Saxonism. *"C'est produit,"* she said, imparting the knowledge to us in a whisper, "by vibr-rating the uvula!"

During the next week, we sat there, like forty purring Renaults, vibrating our uvulas.

Enfin came Verlaine, with his tears. As a supreme exercise, we were to learn to declaim a poem by one of the famous harmonists of France, and we were to do it entirely by ear. (At this time, we knew the meaning of not one word except *"ici!"* with which, carefully admonished to chirp "œp not down!" we had been taught to answer the roll.) Years later, when I could *read* French, I came upon the poem in its natural state. To my surprise, it looked like this:

> *Il pleure dans mon coeur*
> *Comme il pleut sur la ville.*
> *Quelle est cette langueur*
> *Qui pénètre mon coeur?*
>
> *O bruit doux de la pluie*
> *Par terre . . .*

And so on. But the way it is engraved on my heart, my ear, and my uvula is something else again. As hour after hour, palm to breast, wrist to brow, we moaned like a bevy of Ulalumes, making the exquisite distinction between *"pleure"* and *"pleut,"* sounding our "r" like cat women, and dropping "l"s liquid as bulbuls, what we saw in our mind's eye was this:

> il plœ:r dã mõ kœ:r
> k m il pl syr la vij
> k l s t lãgœ:r
> ki pen tr mõ kœ:r
>
> o bryi du d la plyi
> par te:r . . .

And *so* on.

Late in the term, Mme. Cécile Sorel paid New York a visit, and Mlle. Girard took us to see her in *La Dame aux Camélias*. Sorel's tea gowns and our own romantic sensibilities helped us to get some of her phthisic story. But what we marvelled at most was that she sounded exactly like us.

L'envoi comes somewhat late—twenty years later—but, like the tragic flaw of the Greeks what Mlle. G. had planted so irrevocably was bound to show up in a last act somewhere. I went to France.

During the interim, I had resigned myself to the fact that although I had "had" French so intensively—for Mlle. G. had continued to be just as exacting all the way through grammar, *dictée*, and the rest of it—I still did not seem to "have" it. In college, my accent had earned me a brief eminence, but, of course, we did not spend much time speaking French, this being regarded as a frivolous addiction, the pursuit of which had best be left to the Berlitz people or to tacky parlor groups presided over by stranded foreign widows in need of funds. As for vocabulary or idiom, I stood with Racine on my right hand and Rimbaud on my left—a *cordon-bleu* cook who had never been taught how to boil an egg. Across the water, there was presumably a nation, *obscurcie de miasmes humains*, that used its own speech for purposes of asking the way to the bathroom, paying off porters, and going shopping, but for me the language remained the vehicle of de Vigny, Lamartine, and Hugo, and France a murmurous orchestral country where the *cieux* were full of *clarté*, the oceans sunk in *ombres profondes*, and where the most useful verbs were *souffler* and *gémir*.

On my occasional encounters with French visitors, I would apologize, in a few choicely carved phrases that always brought compliments, for being out of practice, after which I retired—into English if *they* had *it,* into the next room if they hadn't. Still, when I sailed, it was with hope—based on the famous accent—that in France I would somehow speak French. If I had only known, it would have been far better to go, as an underprivileged friend of mine did, armed with the one phrase her husband had taught her— "*Au secours!*"

Arriving at my small hotel in Paris, I was met by the owner, M. Lampacher, who addressed me in arrogantly correct English. When we had finished our arrangements in that language, I took the plunge. *"Merci!"* I said. It came out just lovely, the "r" like treacle, the "ci" not down but œp.

"Ah, Madame!" he said. "You speak French."

I gave him the visitors' routine.

"You mock, Madame. You have the accent *absolument pur.*"

The next morning, I left the hotel early for a walk around Paris. I had not been able to understand the boy who brought me breakfast, but no doubt he was from the provinces. Hoping that I would not encounter too many people from the provinces, I set out. I tramped for miles, afloat upon the first beatific daze of tourism. One by one, to sounds as of northern lights popping and sunken cathedrals emerging, all the postcards were coming true, and it was not until I was returning on the bus from Chaillot that, blinking, I listened for the first time that day.

Two women opposite me were talking; from their glances, directed at my plastic rain boots, they were talking about me. I was piqued at their apparent assumption that I would not understand them. A moment later, listening with closed eyes, I was glad that they could not be aware of the very odd way in which I was not understanding them. For what I was hearing went something like this: "r g rd l merik n se kout*f* u s kōn bl s n sp purl s bl ō povw rlesulje"

Il Plœ:r Dā Mō Kœ:r

" l n sōpavremāa ʃik lezamerik n ʃakynr sālalotr"
"a wi [Pause] tykon mari la fijœl d mō d mi fr r ādre s lwi [or s l] av k l buk tylarākōtre ʃemwa alo:r lœdi swa;r l [or il] a f t yn foskuʃ"

Hours later, in my room, with the help of the dictionary and Mlle. G.'s training in *dictée*, I pieced together what they had said. It seemed to have been roughly this: *"Regarde, l'Américaine, sescaoutchoucs. C'est convenable, ça, n'est-ce-pas, pour l'ensemble. On peut voir les souliers."*

"Ah, elles ne sont pas vraiment chics, les Américaines. Chacune ressemble à l'autre."

"Ah, oui. [Pause] *Tu connais Marie, la filleule de mon demi-frère André—celui [or il] a fait une fausse couche!"*

One of them, then, had thought my boots convenient for the ensemble, since one could see the shoes; the other had commented on the lack of real chic among American women, who all resembled one another. Digressing, they had gone on to speak of Marie, the goddaughter of a stepbrother, "the one with the *bouc*. You have met him [or her, since one could not tell from the construction] at my house." Either he or Marie had made a false couch, whatever that was.

The latter I could not find in the dictionary at all. *"Bouc"* I at first recalled as *"banc"*—either André or Marie had some kind of bench, then, or pew. I had just about decided that André had a seat in the Chamber of Deputies and had made some kind of political mistake, when it occured to me that the word had been *"bouc"*—goatee—which almost certainly meant André. What had he done? Or Marie? What the hell did it mean "to make a false couch"?

I sat for the good part of an hour, freely associating—really, now, the goddaughter of a stepbrother! When I could bear it no longer, I rang up an American friend who had lived in Paris for some years, with whom I was to lunch the next day.

"Oh, yes, how are you?" said Ann.

"Dead tired, actually," I said, "and I've had a slight shock. Listen, it seems I can't speak French at all. Will you translate something?"

"Sure"

"What does to *'faire une fausse couche'* mean?"

"Honey!" said Ann.

"What?"

"Where are you, dear?" she said, in a low voice. "At a doctor's?"

"No, for God's sake. I'm at the hotel. What's the matter with you? You're as bad as the dictionary."

"Nothing's the matter with me," said Ann. "The phrase just means 'to have a miscarriage,' that's all."

"Ohhh," I said. "Then it was Marie after all. Poor Marie."

"Are you all right?"

"Oh, I'm fine," I said. "Just fine. And thanks. I'll see you tomorrow."

I went to bed early, assuring myself that what I had was merely disembarkation jitters (what would the psychologists call it—transliteration syndrome?), which would disappear overnight. Otherwise it was going to be very troublesome having to retire from every conversation to work it out in symbols.

A month went by, and the syndrome had not disappeared. Now and then, it was true, the more familiar nouns and verbs did make their way straight to my brain, by-passing the tangled intermediaries of my ear and the International Phonetic Alphabet. Occasionally, I was able to pick up an unpoetically useful phrase: to buy a brassière you asked for "something to hold up the gorge with"; the French said "Couci-couça" (never *"Comme ci, comme ça"*) and, when they wanted to say "I don't know," turned up their palms and said "Schpuh." But meanwhile, my accent, fed by the lilt of true French, altogether outsoared the shadow of my night. When I did dare the phrases prepared carefully in my room for the eventualities of the day, they fell so superbly that any French vis-à-vis immediately dropped all thought of giving me a handicap and addressed me in the native argot, at the native rate—leaving me struck dumb.

New Year's Eve was my last night in Paris. I had planned to fly to London to start the new year with telephones, parties, the wireless, conversation, in a wild blaze of unrestricted communication. But the airport had informed me that no planes were flying the Channel, or perhaps anywhere, for the next twenty-four hours, New

Year's Eve being the one night on which the pilots were traditionally "allowed" to get drunk. At least, it seemed to me that I had been so informed, but perhaps I libel, for by now my passion for accurately understanding what was said to me was dead. All my pockets and purses were full of paper scraps of decoding, set down in vowel-hallucinated corners while my lips moved grotesquely, and it seemed to me that, if left alone here any longer, I would end by having composed at random a phonetic variorum for France.

In a small, family-run café around the corner from my hotel, where I had often eaten alone, I ordered dinner, successive *cafés filtres*, and repeated doses of marc. Tonight, at the elegiac opening of the new year, it was "allowed"—for pilots and the warped failures of educational snobbism—to get drunk. Outside, it was raining, or weeping; in my heart, it was doing both.

Presently, I was the only customer at any of the zinc tables. Opposite, in a corner, the *grand-père* of the family of owners lit a Gauloise and regarded me with the privileged stare of the elderly. He was the only one there who seemed aware that I existed; for the others I had the invisibility of the foreigner who cannot "speak"— next door to that of a child, I mused, except for the adult password of money in the pocket. The old man's daughter, or daughter-in-law, a dark woman with a gall-bladder complexion and temperament, had served me obliquely and retired to the kitchen, from which she emerged now and then to speak sourly to her husband, a capped man, better-looking than she, who ignored her, lounging at the bar like a customer. I should have liked to know whether her sourness was in her words as well as her manner, and whether his lordliness was something personal between them or only the authority of the French male, but their harsh gutturals, so far from the sugarplum sounds I had been trained to that they did not even dissolve into phonetics, went by me like the crude blue smoke of the Gauloise. A girl of about fourteen—their daughter, I thought— was tending bar and deflecting the remarks of the customers with a petted, precocious insouciance. Now and then, her parents addressed remarks, either to her or to the men at the bar, that seemed to have the sharpness of reprimand, but I could not be sure; to my eye the gaiety of the men toward the young girl had a certain avuncular decorum that made the scene pleasant and tender to watch. In my own country, I loved to listen at bars, where the human scene was often arrested as it is in those genre paintings whose deceptively simple contours must be approached with all one's knowledge of the period, and it saddened me not to be able to savor those nuances here.

I lit a Gauloise, too, with a flourish that the old man, who nodded stiffly, must have taken for a salute. And why not? Pantomime was all that was left to me. Or money. To hell with my perfectionist urge to understand; I must resign myself to being no different from those summer thousands who jammed the ocean every June, to whom Europe was merely a montage of their own sensations, a glamorous old phoenix that rose seasonally, just for them. On impulse, I mimed an invitation to the old man to join me in a marc. On second thought, I signaled for marc for everybody in the house.

"To the new year!" I said, in French, waving my glass at the old man. Inside my brain, my monitor tapped his worried finger—did *"nouvelle"* come before or after *"année"* in such cases, and wasn't the accent a little "ice cream"? I drowned him, in another marc.

Across the room from me, the old man's smile faded in and out like the Cheshire cat's; I was not at all surprised when it spoke, in words I seemed to understand, inquiring politely as to my purpose in Paris. I was here on a scholarship, I replied. I was a writer. (*"Ecrivain? Romancier?"* asked my monitor faintly.)

"Ah," said the old man. "I am familiar with one of your writers. Père Le Buc."

"Père Le Buc?" I shook my head sadly. "I regret, but it is not known to me, the work of the Father Le Buc."

"Pas un homme!" he said. *"Une femme! Une femme qui s'appelle Père Le Buc!"*

My monitor raised his head for one last time. "P rl byk!" he chirped desperately. "P rl byk!"

I listened. "Oh, my God," I said then. "Of course. That is how it would be. Pearl Buck!"

"Mais oui," said the old man, beaming and raising his glass. "P rl byk!"

At the bar, the loungers, thinking we were exchanging some toast, raised their own glasses in courteous imitation. "P rl byk!" they said, politely. "P rl byk!"

I raised mine. *"Il pleure,"* I began, *"il pleure dans mon coeur comme il pleut . . ."*

Before the evening was over, I had given them quite a selection: from Verlaine, from Heredia's "Les Trophées," from Baudelaire's poem on a painting by Delacroix, from de Musset's "R-r-rappelletoi!" As a final tribute, I gave them certain stanzas from Hugo's "L'Expiation"—the ones that begin *"Waterloo! Waterloo! Waterloo! Morne plaine!"* And in between, raised or lowered by a new faith that was not all brandy, into an air freed of cuneiform at last I spoke French.

Making my way home afterward, along the dark stretches of the Rue du Bac, I reflected that to learn a language outside its native habitat you must really believe that the other country exists—in its humdrum, its winter self. Could I remember to stay there now—down in that lower-case world in which stairs creaked, cops yelled, in which women bought brassières and sometimes made the false couch?

The door of my hotel was locked. I rang, and M. Lampacher admitted me. He snapped on the stair light, economically timed to go out again in a matter of seconds, and watched me as I mounted the stairs with the aid of the banister.

"Off bright and early, hmm?" he said sleepily, in French. "Well, good night, Madame. Hope you had a good time here."

I turned, wanting to answer him properly, to answer them all. At that moment, the light went off, perhaps to reinforce forever my faith in the mundanity of France.

"Ah, ça va, ça va!" I said strongly, into the dark. "Couci-couça. Schpuh."

Madame Broulard

EVAN S. CONNELL

Apartments in Paris sometimes explode, even so they are better than hotel rooms. For a number of weeks after my arrival I lived in a hotel near the Seine. The room was quite long and narrow, tapering like a coffin, was papered with orange fleurs-de-lis, and with its medieval window closed smelled like a rabbit hutch. During those weeks I knew only one person in Paris, an American college friend who had been in the city about three years working for the U.S. Government, and when he telephoned one morning to say I might possibly get an apartment—not much, he cautioned, but an apartment—I told him several times that I would take it. A friend of the French family he had lived with when he first arrived had decided to rent her place. On the phone he advised not being too eager or she would increase the price, but I was very eager indeed and told him that if the price went up I would do without a noon meal in order to get the place. Apparently he had never lived in a room lined with orange fleurs-de-lis because he did not sound sympathetic; all he said was to meet him at the Pasteur metro stop about 6:30.

Madame Broulard was also at the metro stop though I did not know it at the time; I noticed only a woman of perhaps forty-five with extremely coarse red hair and a complexion like cork who strolled back and forth swinging a black handbag and stopping often to look at sweets in a bakery window. I assumed she was a prostitute.

Presently Max emerged from the underground station. He was carrying in one hand a green fish net full of lettuce and onions, two empty wine bottles and some American PX toilet paper, and in the other hand a brief case of painted Italian leather. While in Paris he had grown a thin, snarled beard but otherwise was unchanged from the days when he had been inter-collegiate pole-vaulting champion. He saw us both at the same time; with a crisscross nod he indicated to each of us who the other was.

"*Enchantée, monsieur,*" said Madame Broulard, smiling at me and holding up, either to shake or kiss, a freckled white hand that felt like a chicken breast.

At the time I spoke textbook French, a language most Parisians profess not to understand, yet her smile remained brave when I carefully pronounced a return greeting. While we walked the several blocks to her apartment she and Max talked steadily and too rapidly for me to understand.

The apartment was a seventh-floor walk-up and consisted of a cordon of rooms which became smaller, darker and more mysterious the farther one proceeded, terminating in a kitchen-bathroom where it was necessary to switch on the light. The front room had six thick red draperies which swept the floor and sometimes stirred as though people were hiding behind them. I suggested to Max that Poe must have lived and created some of his ghouls in these chambers. Madame Broulard understood no English but caught the name of Poe and exclaimed that *La Chute de la Maison Usher* was formidable.

The walls of the second room were massed with what may have been the dingiest collection of pictures in the world—sepia and gray Fragonard-ish prints which appeared to have been placed on the roof every time it rained, as well as a number of those stiff Virgins painted on cracked wood which summer tourists buy at the Clignancourt flea market and take proudly home to Kansas City or to the Bronx. There was also a reclining nude with a skin of rancid butter. Madame clearly was fond of this picture. She asked Max a short question and he said to me, "Does the picture offend you? Tell her it's beautiful."

I said, *"Tres belle!"*

"Don't overdo it," said Max.

We went on for a look at the kitchen-bathroom. This contained the tub, over which a boxlike gas heater was suspended, the toilet, stove, bidet, washbasin, a big medicine cabinet (on the way Max had remarked, "She thinks she has liver trouble. Everybody in France thinks he has liver trouble.") and a coil of pipes on the underside of which hung concentric circles of stalactites. There was also the electric meter, a trash carton, a porcelain coffee grinder with cherubs painted by madame, a frosted window, and what I took to be a bird cage but which proved to be the thing they put lettuce in after it is washed. They then hold this cage out the window, said Max, and angrily swing it around and around and the water is hurled off, splattering on the ledges of all the windows below. These were the larger objects in the kitchen; shelves and recesses contained rows of pots and condiments and labeled bottles.

I leaned across the bathtub and looked from under the water heater out the window: there was the Eiffel Tower. I had known all along I wanted this apartment, now it was foolish to pretend any longer.

Max told her I would very much like an apartment where one could take a bath while looking at the Eiffel Tower. She thought this a rather peculiar reason but was pleased that I was pleased. She made a pretense of considering but unquestionably she wanted the rent money as much as I wanted to get out of my hotel. The price was 15,000 francs, truly reasonable. Max said that by admiring the nude I had probably saved myself 5,000 francs. Madame, however, gave another reason for the price: she had never rented before and was more interested in finding a sober, respectful tenant than in making lots of money. I said to tell her I would take good care of her property, that I drank little, and would be reading most of the time. The fact that I was a student pleased her and so before long it was agreed that I might move in whenever I wished. An hour later I returned with my suitcases.

I decided to begin my stay in Madame Broulard's apartment with a bath. Remembering instructions given me on the operation of the heater, I first pulled open the drawer and lighted the pilot, then closed the drawer and after making certain that the little flame had not gone out I sat on the edge of the tub and began to open the tap. Finally the water came into being, a few drops leaked from the nozzle, a trickle, and when the handle had been cranked until it wobbled there could be seen a flow about the size of a baby's finger. Yet the gas had not ignited. I continued leisurely twisting the handle; at the time I had not learned that one turns this handle furiously. To turn it slowly is to allow gas seepage. I was gazing at the Eiffel Tower when the gas exploded. It was rather like diving off a springboard and landing flat. The blast moved a cup and saucer several inches along the drainboard. A few seconds later when I had recovered from the shock the gas was roaring and the nozzle spitting steam.

The same afternoon Madame Broulard returned. I thought she must have forgotten something, but her manner was vague. I could not guess what she wanted. I poured two glasses of wine and offered her a chair. She brought out a paper and pencil. After a while I understood that she wished to make an inventory of the silverware. She was embarrassed but after all she did not know me, she said—though I thought her three-year acquaintance with Max should be sufficient security—and it was therefore quite necessary to mark down the number of pieces. I would then sign the paper. Clearly the silver was valuable; I did not understand all she said about it, which was considerable, but gathered that it had belonged to her family for generations and could never be replaced. So, taking our wineglasses and paper and pencil, we walked into the back room where she opened the polished wood chest and began laying out the pattern. Un. Deux. Trois. Quatre . . . And so on through the teaspoons and the snail forks and then into the butter knives. We were about half through this set when she folded the paper, slipped it into her purse and with a smile said all this was unnecessary. Taking our wine, we returned to the front room and conversation, but she was not at ease and finished her glass quickly and said she was sorry to have deranged me. The silver of her *grandpère*, she was positive, would be secure in my hands. I told her it would be. Was there anything I needed? No, I replied as best I could, the apartment was fine and I was very content to be in such a place. I did not see her again until an evening in late November.

She came by about dusk. I poured two more glasses of wine and we sat down for a chat. She asked if I were enjoying Paris, if I had been to the opera and to the Comédie Française and if I had made the trip to Chartres to see the famous cathedral. We talked for possibly an hour. She found my French improved and gave me a lesson in the correct pronunciation of the letter *r*.

Eventually she mentioned the necessity for visiting the toilet, the cabinet as they delicately put the matter, and having excused herself, she disappeared into the back rooms. The lid of the silver chest creaked as she lifted it.

A moment afterward came the sound of the toilet chain, of the door opening and closing, and Madame reappeared rubbing her hands as though she had just finished washing them. We drank another glass of wine. Was there anything I needed for the apartment? No. Could she do anything at all for me? No, I said, I was well satisfied; the quarters pleased me. I then recalled having broken one of her champagne goblets and asked if I could pay for it, or if not, where I might find a replacement, but she threw aside her hands, exclaiming that the goblet was nothing. In renting, she continued, one must expect a certain breakage and I was not to let the matter worry me.

At the door she said, *"Bon soir, monsieur. Vous êtes trop gentil."* And I also said good evening and that she was very agreeable.

The next time Madame Broulard visited was at my invitation after an accident in the kitchen. The washbasin had been cracked before I moved in; a streak like the photographic negative of a lightning bolt ran down one slope, across the bottom and up the opposite side. If water stood in the bowl long enough a few drops would seep through and form a puddle on the floor. It had been that way, she had remarked when Max and I first looked at the place, for twenty-two years—Monsieur Broulard had dropped a syphon bottle and created the crack. But as it was not serious and she felt plumber's fees to be outrageous the basin had never been fixed. I had paid no attention to it other than not allowing water to stand, but apparently the crack had weakened the bottom. I was washing a sweater when the basin, too, exploded. Now a porcelain washbasin does not break like a china plate or a drinking glass, it goes off like a light bulb dropped on a concrete floor. All at once a bucket under the basin was full of porcelain shards and I was reaching through a jagged hole. My shirt sleeves were ripped as if they had been sliced with razors and both arms were badly scraped.

As I did not know how to contact Madame Broulard at that hour of the evening and as neither Max nor I had a telephone I took the metro to his place near Montmartre. He was entertaining some artist friends. I told him about the accident and said I would replace the basin but that Madame should probably be notified. He said he would call her in the morning from his office; for the present I should join the party. I knew very little about art but he said the same was true of artists. He introduced me around the living room where everybody was on the floor—a collage of plaid shirts, hairy arms, sandals, girls' legs, and many blue packets of Gauloises cigarettes. Max and I then went into the kitchen where he had been uncorking bottles.

"How are you and Madame getting along?" he asked. "She's unreasonable sometimes, you know. She's been that way since the war."

I said that we'd had a nice talk the time she stopped by. She found me droll and genteel. I mailed a check for the rent on the first of every month and a few days later always got a pleasant acknowledgment written by her employer in eighteenth-century English. I didn't know anything about her life during the war.

"Her husband was killed. He was starting to walk across the Boulevard des Capucines when a German lance corporal shot him in the testicles. I shouldn't think that would be a fatal wound but anyway Monsieur Broulard died, maybe from heartbreak. Madame could never find out why he was shot. Nobody ever knew why. Nobody ever does." Max had been getting red and swollen as he pulled at a cork. He was steadying the bottle between his feet and had one big hand wrapped in a towel. When he finally got the cork out he continued: "Things like that have been going on in Paris for a long time. Paris has always been an occupied city. At present it's us, the Americans with their purple nylon shirts and chewing gum and three-hundred-dollar cameras and American Express tours. Why, in places like Concorde and Pig Alley and over the Champs you can't find a Frenchman on the streets. Before us it was the Germans, and before them somebody else, and so on back to

Hannibal or Attila or whoever it was first knew a good thing when he saw it. Always this city has been dominated by some foreign power. Always."

He popped open another bottle and began twisting the cork off the screw. "Now there was some point I intended to make but I can't think what it was." He finished unscrewing the cork, placed it in line with others that stood in a half-circle atop the stove, and smiled faintly as he remarked, "Perhaps it's this: as long as you're in Paris you've got to realize that you're part of the occupation force. You'll be treated as such. Now let's join the others."

As we entered the front room a fat, bearded sculptor wearing rope sandals was describing Spain. I remembered that his name was Julian and that he was having his first one-man show somewhere in the St. Germain district. He accepted a bottle from Max and shouted: "*Bueno! Bueno, hombre!*"

A few minutes later an English boy who wore a loose black turtleneck sweater and who had been eating peaches turned to me and said, drawing out the words, "I'm David. David. They tell me you have an apartment? Isn't Madame Broulard the libertine!" As to why she was a libertine David continued after folding a peach skin and placing it atop a stack rising from the ash tray. "But Max has told you *why* she's renting, I mean he must have told you . . ." David was annoyed that I hadn't heard. His voice grew sharp. "Because her employer has wearied of the little wife! And imported Madame Broulard! Into his own home. Now think of the children, won't you? I do feel that Parisians are at once the most wonderful and despicable people on earth." He began to lick his fingers while he stared at a dirty Siamese cat that had gone to sleep on the couch.

Several more artists came to the party and they all began talking about a new movement called Fragmentism. An hour or so later, realizing that I had not yet completed a paper that would shortly be due at the Sorbonne, I located Max reading a book in the kitchen. My intention had been to tell him good night. Instead we got to talking of the war, of how it had affected the people we knew. Max said that when the United States dropped the atom bomb he had almost renounced his American citizenship. Almost, he said, but finally he had not. "I don't know," he said, "even now I am not sure what I ought to have done. Civilized people don't destroy cities. No matter how you rationalize it. Speak of Belsen. Speak of Hiroshima."

We could hear Julian's laughter from the front room, and the confused argument that never would end.

"Well," Max said, "I'm like the others. I, too, am terrified and am scratching at life. Attempting to piece together something significant. Take Madame Broulard: her nephew was in the resistance but on his first assignment he became so frightened that he surrendered, not only himself but two others. The Germans tortured and killed all three. Nothing any more is secure or comprehensible to Madame; she is so much alone, trying to hold on to something, anything, that retains a shred of meaning. In America the group announces a pattern for life; in Europe there are not more groups, there are individuals, each in his own way striking out at everything that has wounded him and each in his own time picking from the ashes whatever bagatelle will reassure him."

In the front room a girl shrieked, "Look at the time!" It was, in fact, just eight minutes before one in the morning. The metro stops at one.

We heard David say, "Everybody can sleep here. Max doesn't mind one bit." And there in the kitchen Max smiled.

But in spite of David's invitation the guests began crowding out the door and as they went stumbling down the steep circular staircase in absolute darkness I followed.

Once on the street we all ran for it and inside the station split up without pausing for goodbyes to go our separate directions. I ran alone through an echoing corridor, the wall frames of which had been rented by a mustard company and filled with replicas of the same poster in alternating colors, first in bile and then in mustard. The metro agent at the portillon saw me running toward him just as the last train rumbled into position. He knew I was not French, probably he knew I was American, and he shut the gate a moment before I reached it.

In my best French I asked: "It's the last train?"

"*Oui,*" he said contentedly.

"But then . . ." I protested.

"You're too late, monsieur," he said, gazing beyond me. There was still time for him to open the gate and allow me on the train. I pointed out this fact.

"It's not possible," he said.

There was nothing to be done. He would not let me through although he would have let a Frenchman through. As I started back along the corridor he said politely, *"Bonsoir, monsieur."*

I turned around to look at him. His face was expressionless.

Several blocks away there was a taxi stand. I got in the first cab and gave my address. We drove for perhaps a half mile along the Seine. Here and there on the barges a light could be seen, and the bridges reflected in the water, and I was thinking of what Max had told me.

At the corner of Pasteur and Lecourbe I got out. The meter read 320 francs. I would tip the driver thirty francs. I counted out four one-hundred notes and asked for fifty change. He dropped a large gold coin in my palm and I had walked off several steps before realizing it was not heavy enough. It was a gilded two-franc. He was drawing away from the curb when I ran into the street, caught the handle and jerked open the door. He stopped the taxi and I met the bland face of the metro agent.

The argument about the fraudulent coin began but I was angry by this time, more angry than he, and in addition I had no other change in my pockets, so at last he admitted he might possibly have given me the counterfeit. He was apologetic, examining the coin and shaking his head. He would report this thing to the police, this swindling. He gave me a genuine fifty-franc piece, selecting it from a handful not quite concealed of gilded two-francs.

Madame Broulard appeared the following morning with such an anxious look that I suspected Max had embellished the story of the accident. I showed her the basin and demonstrated how it happened. But had I not been injured? Well, my arms were a bit swollen and stiff. She must have a look at them. Oh, this was terrible. No, Madame, it's nothing. Nothing. At last we got back to the basin. She was unable to believe it could have happened. Americans astonished her. They were savages. No Frenchman would ever have an accident like that. Never.

Although the bowl had been cracked to begin with she had used it for twenty-two years and I was certain she could have made it last that much longer, therefore it seemed I should pay the cost of replacement; however, she reminded me of the crack and in the end we decided to divide the cost.

She came back the following Monday with news that it would cost altogether 20,000 francs. I knew that 10,000 would be difficult for her, but she only smiled and with her hands inadvertently outlined a butterfly. At such moments she was no longer a coarsely red-haired woman with limbs rather like mushroom stalks but one of the legendary Parisiennes, a proper descendant of Maintenon and Sévigne.

Before she left I told her that the following month would be my last in Paris. My year of study abroad was complete and I would be going home. She was intensely interested in the United States and began asking about my home and my plans and before she left I had brought out snapshots of the house and my sister's baby and the cocker spaniel pups. When I first moved into the apartment I had admired a tiny wood Franciscan who sat brooding among the yellowing paperbound editions of Maupassant and Baudelaire; now she hurried across to it and said I must take it to remember her by. Although I protested she would not listen; she put it into my pocket. I complained that I had nothing to offer in return, and she threw out her hands in despair, a moment later saying I should send her a snapshot of myself before the Statue of Liberty. This would be simple enough because the boat would go past it into New York Harbor.

"It is from us to you, this statue," she told me, and I said I knew and that all Americans knew of the good wishes of France.

At the door she said once again how desolate she was that I must leave, how she hoped my stay had been pleasant. She would try to come by on the morning of my departure but her boss was formidable, *un véritable tigre*, and so it would be doubtful. If not, then I could simply leave the keys with the concierge, and if I failed to write from America she would never forgive me.

It seemed during those final weeks in Paris that I was living in Utrillo's city—from the street of the agile rabbit to the pale nipple of the church of Sacré Coeur, and the olive-green book boxes propped open along the *quai* to the sienna chimney pipes high on the mansard roofs. The sun, large now for summer, patinaed walks and grilles and glinted on metal vases bolted to plaques inscribed, *Ici Est Tombé Pour La France* ... followed by a name, a date, and nothing more.

The veritable tiger of a boss gave Madame Broulard part of the morning off on the day I was to leave. Shortly before noon she arrived carrying a black satchel like a doctor's instrument bag and she put all the silver in it, excepting a knife and a fork and a teaspoon which I was to use for my lunch.

She said, "I have been wanting to have it cleaned for such a long time." She zipped up this bag, placed it by the door and turned to me with a smile. "At what hour does your train depart?" It was to leave for Le Havre late in the afternoon. "And you will write to me from New York? I'll worry because the sea, they say, is so rough this time of year." We talked a few minutes more and then we shook hands and I promised to leave the key with the concierge downstairs. "Then, monsieur," she told me, smiling a little sadly, "goodbye. I am so sorry you must go." And taking up her bag she started briskly down the stairs.

Max had recently bought a jeep and was driving me to the station. I heard the tires and next the horn; he was late as always. I had been waiting almost an hour, sitting with three pieces of silverware in my hand, wondering what to do. I had thought of hiding them somewhere in the apartment, perhaps behind one of the sepia etchings where she would never think of hunting, then in a month or so sending her a postcard revealing where they could be found, but I remembered Max saying that in this crucified land human hope and reassurance take unaccustomed forms, therefore I only washed them and carefully dried them and placed them in a row on the exact center of the table—one knife and one fork and one silver spoon.

The Waiting Room

Joan Frank

Rita Carr came to Paris when her marriage of fourteen years had ended and with it, her job.

It was a long-term mistake, she liked to say, and there was nothing for it now but to begin again, if you can call it beginning when you're a little past the middle, she thought—when you are forty-six. Saying the number aloud, in a voice that quavered only slightly, she thought herself decisive, and daring. People dodged having to say the numbers now, she noticed, because in spite of everyone knowing better, the advanced number was like an embarrassing score, or a statement of the progression of a virulent disease.

Rita could say the number if she was asked, which happened sort of obliquely She would be asked it in roundabout ways by women she invited to lunch, women she had hoped to develop as friends. But when she obliged their directness with her daring honesty it seemed to discomfit them—they looked around the room and spoke quickly of other matters, and tended not to initiate engagements after that unless she prodded and dogged them. She would feel a bit chaotic, uncertain how she'd offended, then decide it was her imagination, and put that woman's name on her list of must-see's. Rita was tall, had pale skin, faint red eyebrows, and slightly protruding, pale blue eyeballs; one of those female faces that seem a blank slate before makeup—a face that if she made it up properly and had a decent amount of sleep and not eaten too much candy the day before, could look actually pretty, pretty in that almost-model way you see of women out to dinner, in restaurants with velvet on the walls. Untended, Rita's rinsed-auburn hair seemed to sit too far back on her scalp, like a mannequin's slipped wig. But with a good haircut and the right moisturizer and a pleasant, indirect light, and of course some serious organizing of clothes and belts and costume jewelry, she could look almost mysteriously desirable It was hard work. Rita had big feet, and a gap between her two front teeth.

The man to whom Rita had been married, a doughy, balding fellow with the habit of working a toothpick around one side of his mouth, had finally agreed to buy out her half of the little radio station. The marriage, she later told me, was something she had done the way many people undertake marriage, for lack at the time of anything better to do. Rita took a temp job as a receptionist for a winery in the Napa Valley, and when the local college advertised a Paris semester, she gathered up her buyout money and signed on, with the idea she might purvey her experience with the vineyards and never come back to America.

Rita had no French. It was the first trip she had taken in the fourteen years since she'd married. The program set her up in a dorm room in the fourteenth district, near the Place d'Italie. It was a pleasant enough neighborhood, wide streets lined with blank-faced apartment blocks, the métro stop bubbling up a steady stream of students and housewives and commuters like an underground spring. But the problem of language at first exhausted Rita, and for a few days she felt heavy and slept a lot, rarely leaving the dorm. Every time she set foot outside the building—a great, glassed-in affair with enormous tour buses crouched out front, farting black exhaust straight into the doors and windows—just to buy a sandwich, or a bottle of wine or a sack of cookies meant a terrible struggle, and her face would flame as she fought to concentrate on counting out the right number of francs for the bitterly contemptuous clerks at the checkout counters. All they had to hear was a single je voudrais in her Oklahoma drawl, the r's round and slurry, to press their lips into a bloodless line and turn away as if she'd never been standing there. She relied for a while on the dorm's cafeteria, where the personnel (young French students, one eye on their open textbooks as they doled up overcooked cauliflower) had at least a flickering comprehension of English and a longer tolerance for her twangy American stammer. It was colder that winter than anything she had felt for a long time; snowing on and off in paperweight swirls. She often sat for hours in the dorm's foyer, writing carefully chipper postcards to people she did not miss, drinking expensive coffees.

Rita tried for a time to befriend the other students in her program. They were mostly women of eighteen and nineteen, daughters of retired aerospace workers with neat tract homes nestled in green suburbs; daughters whose trust funds stipulated that certain checks might be cut before the age of maturity, only for educational endeavors. These were big boned, big-breasted girls who spent every day making up carefully and blow drying before heading out to St. Michel and the Opéra to shop and shop and shop. They seemed to have decided the best way to make themselves felt in the city was to strike bored-princess poses: complaining to Rita about being heckled in the métro stops and streets; feigning insouciance about the great roaring Gothic majesty and filth and impossible centuries of dripping history around them—"It's only a city," one had sniffed. In fact on arrival the young women had become briskly practical, mastering their awe as well as the métro system, shifting into a cool-huntress determination, a singleness of purpose that might be read on their faces if one looked twice: to get a French lover. The girls were polite to Rita, but they always seemed to find reasons to be unable to meet her for dinner or a drink or a walk. Rita had a creeping, rancid sense, watching them look nervously past her in the dorm lobby or along the adjacent Boulevard St. Jacques (where Americans could spot one another from blocks away by their strapping size, the fulsome flesh on their bones)—that the young women felt that to be seen standing near her would spoil their image, and their luck.

    Rita enrolled in the college's French instruction, but it was taught by an old woman whose eyes swam like trapped fish behind her thick lenses. Madame Bergeron—while very sweet—never appeared quite sure what was supposed to happen next; it was like crawling through narrow tunnels to try to apply the half-wit phraseology of Madame's lessons to the furious world of Parisian vernacular. The speech of daily transactions seemed to whip past Rita like the thin roar of the TGVs, the grande vitesse trains that streamed over the countryside. Rita had glimpsed these bullet-shaped trains sitting in rows, in the big echoey stations, and thought about them at night, in her skinny bunk bed, the streetlight a milky cataract through the dirty window glass. She even fancied her tiny dorm room was shaped like a train's sleeping car. One day, because she had money for it, because the guidebooks called it pleasant and because it was relatively near, she bought a ticket to Orléans. I was surprised at how sorry I felt for Rita just after this event, and unaccountably, how repelled; I had an idea then what had occurred with her lunch partners. I was teaching with another college housed in the dorm that winter, and she had cornered me one morning in the coffee bar, presumably because I was an American, a woman closer to her in age, and—I am sure she hoped—in sympathies. But I was overloaded that semester with too much grading, and too little unstructured time in the city (perhaps the only time I have been relieved to float the truth of that situation as an excuse). I apologized that I'd rarely have a free moment; thus, the reports she began to offer of what followed, necessarily came in the form of short summations.

It began with the trip to Orléans.

It was late February, freezing, and the sky and land seemed saturated with the grays of the millennia of winters that had gone before. Mist covered the country, but Rita made herself study the outlines of suburbs and farmhouses gliding past, congratulating herself for her decisiveness. Orléans, it turned out, was a not unpleasant town, with its requisite tourism office, its Peruvian musicians on the station step—but a town that declared itself and was over, for her distracted purposes, too quickly She walked to the cathedral—stone interior emanating currents of stunningly cold breath; a crypt must be warmer, she thought—to the various statues of Jeanne d'Arc, with their florid inscriptions, to the art gallery, which by comparison with the Disneyland bedlam of the Louvre, seemed unnervingly empty on a weekday afternoon. She watched yuppie wives pushing babies in expensive strollers, students languishing in billows of their own smoky exhalations, elderly women squinting at the market-stall vegetables. She wandered the centre ville, with its concentric circles of wealth—Gucci and St. Laurent outlets at center, Monoprix and shabbier brasseries on the next orbiting ring, little Asian cafés next, and so on. And suddenly there was nothing left to do in Orléans, unless she waited for a matinee.

Rita's face and words reflected a constant, slow astonishment —even in retrospect—as she told me about standing on the track, unable to make out the blurred, nasal announcements of departing trains, her stomach fluttering as she stepped onto what she was in no way sure was the right train. And as soon as it pulled out and was gaining smooth speed, she stammered her question to a bored-looking kid reading a computer magazine, and at his disgusted response her stomach completed its fall. She was heading the wrong way, further out into the country, and now she would have to wait and renegotiate a return to Paris from the next stop. It was so hard, so hard. Her head hurt and her eyes ached. She had plopped down opposite the curt young man, leaned her head back against the blue Naugahyde, and in the process of closing her eyes saw the conductor emerging at the other end of the car.

He was a young man, perhaps in his early thirties, and even in her exhaustion she had no trouble noticing he was good-looking. Of medium height, dark eyes—Italianate, the way velvet pupil and iris meshed—and soft brown hair set off by the navy of his uniform and cap. (Why did Frenchmen always have such good hair?) He noticed her at once, and also at once seemed alarmed by his own straying gaze: before it could embarrass him he had yanked it away and was steering it along its professional rounds—but it kept escaping and flitting back at her, for fractions of instants. Messieurs dames, he murmured, and people went about their bored proffering of paper, and he about his punching and inspecting, in the dignified and weary movements that seem to tie French lives together like connect-the-dots drawings: war, love, death, birth; heroism, treachery—all first requiring proper tickets, proper validation.

The two kept wary track of each other as he made his way through the car, and when he stopped at her side she became aware she felt short of breath. When she looked up at approximately the moment he stood next to her, she fancied she saw eagerness, shyness, and a certain amusement jostling for position upon those handsome features.

"You have problem," he said in English.

"Yes," she said, coloring. She tried, in pained French, to describe her mistake, but he cut her off. "Bon: I tell you. You go when I say." And at the first stop he appeared, nodding to her and motioning her to follow him down from the car. Slicing sideways through the commuters in raincoats huddled around the yellow departures display, he made emphatic motions at the line naming the next express for Paris. He pointed as if to underscore its platform number, and looked hard at her. "C'est noté?" he demanded, touching his own eye, and jerking his head toward the billboard display, as if he were drilling a vexingly slow pupil for an exam and her grade was to directly reflect on his honor. "You see?"

She saw. She caught her train, but not before she had given Alain Lemieux her dorm's address and telephone and learned that he lived in Reims, in an apartment loaned to employees of the railroad, while he looked for permanent housing. He was separated, he said, with no telephone, and he worked rotating shifts. But he would call her.

When Rita told me this story I managed to hide an immediate sense of dread; what Americans call (looking meaningfully at you) a bad feeling. Who has not, by now, listened to some poor creature rattle on like the marked animal you already see her to be, and who has not tried, against fierce instinct, to persuade oneself of one's own overbright reassurances? Occasionally it appears we are given the task of simply sitting out the trajectories of people's emergencies, just so we can attend the inevitable call—like ambulances parked around the block: playing cards, eating sandwiches.

Rita had to walk carefully home through the icy gray that day (for the streets were slippery) with her slow and agitated thoughts, her plans to change everything. The list scrolled before her: a new outfit, a better coiffure; she could splurge for a tiny vial of real French perfume; perhaps even join that health club with the fake beach, where all her young costudents went to preen. And as she plotted and assembled her arsenal of persuasions, she waited for Alain's call.

It came in three days. Lurching over their words, they arranged to meet the following Saturday at the Luxembourg Gardens; they would walk to rue Vavin for coffee. The day was, as usual, freezing; all color leached from the close sky, the squat shrubs waiting. Alain stood by the fountain, which was empty and still; one leg propped up on its rim. He wore a collared cotton shirt, thick woolen vest, trousers in the current safari fashion, and a leather jacket. He looked like an ad in Esquire.

"I can't tell you how nice he was," Rita breathed a few days later, as we walked back to the dorm from the metro. We had recognized each other amid the bodies pushing through the exit turnstiles into the cold daylight. When we were free of the crush making our way along St. Jacques in the waning afternoon I questioned her about her first encounter with the young conductor. "He treated me..." She studied the sidewalk, placing her big feet in an odd, tentative gait I had begun to recognize. "—with this incredible delicacy. So polite." She paused again. "Like I was made of glass and jewels."

Of course he did. I asked her what she had learned about him this time.

"Well. We were sitting on these stools, in a bar on the rue Vavin, and got coffees, and he told me—best he could, you know; his English is as rotten as my French," she gave a little har of a laugh, and a glassy grin. "—told me he was trying to find an apartment. He said he'd been married, but that that was over. He didn't seem to want to say much about it," her voice trailed. Alain was curious about Rita's history; asked repeatedly about California. "He said he would like to see me again," she added, glancing sideways at me.

The two had wandered rue Vavin, peering into fragrance shops and baby clothiers, chocolatiers, and picture framers; startled through the window glass by the clerks' thin, even stares, as if the Paris shopkeepers had been dreaming something pleasant until that moment. It was too cold to stay long on the street; Alain said goodbye to her at the Montparnasse stop—this time, he took her hand. He would have to catch a metro to the Gare, and an evening train to Reims. It all seemed too short for Rita; more so since she wasn't sure when their next date would be. Alain was to phone her at the dorm before the week was out. It seemed the train people kept switching his schedules, so he rarely knew in advance when he'd be free. She'd offered several times to phone him at a predesignated spot, but he'd insisted it was not possible. Rita would wait for his call.

She looked at me. "I've already told myself, whatever it turns out to be, I'll just be glad if I can call him a friend." She waited.

I didn't hesitate. "Sure. Certainly. That's the way." In the early stages of these events we have no difficulty believing that we'll be fine with that—that anyone would have no trouble being fine with that.

Two weeks later I found a note from Rita in my dormitory mail, asking me for help composing a letter in French. I rang her room, and agreed to meet her at the coffee bar downstairs. I must explain that my French is never what I wish, but it does bring me the satisfaction of tossing out little mouthfuls of perfunctory phrases like sparkle. As I left my room, I picked up my Larousse de Poche and some paper and seated myself at one of the circular tables amid the rattling dishware and steaming espresso machines; as usual, the young Algerian bartender had turned the rock music up to deafening. Rita appeared after a few minutes. She must have scrubbed her face, for it wore a sheen, perhaps of moisturizer, or those expensive pearlescent lotions women buy. I could detect a too-sweet floral scent. Her eyes were large and her smile enormous, almost goofy, and again I felt that queer combination of sympathy, the wish to reassure her with a vague distaste, a wish to run away. The young women students eyed us as they passed our table, some in fancy trench coats their mothers had bought them, others in cutoff overalls, flight jackets, and hillbilly work boots, thatches of dyed-strawberry hair flopping into their eyes—and in my increasingly odd role as matron-lecturer turned scribe, I nodded them meaningfully along.

"Now then," I turned to Rita. "What's happened?"

Rita's eyes bulged. As their second date, she and Alain had chosen to meet in Vincennes, the pricey suburb just north of the city, where the large hôtels particulires as well as the streets and public squares were named for war generals. Another dirty-ice-colored day They walked the Parc Floral, but it was so cold, they had to imagine the flowers. Finally they gave up on the outdoors and retreated

The Waiting Room

to a brasserie near the metro; they ordered hot brandies. As the liquor warmed them, Rita grew dreamy, and as if he'd ascertained it, Alain chose that exact moment to tell her working his face in an odd way: I have three secrets.

"What on earth," I demanded.

Rita took a breath, and stared into some hidden dimension between us. "He has a child," she began. I made no reaction, and truthfully felt not a morsel of surprise. "A daughter," she went on, looking steadily into the mystery-zone on the tabletop—by the woman he had been married to. Perhaps the girl was ten; Rita wasn't sure she had heard the age correctly. He sees the child once in a while, Alain told Rita.

"That's one," I said.

There was a pause.

"He had a girlfriend for a long time, who hates his wife and does not get along well with the daughter," Rita spoke carefully the way she placed her feet when she walked. "They had a terrible relationship. They screamed at each other, threw things, drove past each other's apartments in the middle of the night to see who might be there—things like that," she said. She kept looking into the air above the table, as if describing tiny holographic scenes gesturing there, visible only to her. "He says he is very glad to be out of it. Well, at least I think he tried to say that," she glanced at me, colored a moment, looked off again.

"That's two," I said.

She looked blank suddenly. "I'm not sure we ever talked about a third," and her voice trailed off again. She seemed to have lost track of the verve and purpose with which she'd sat down—as if these qualities were a frequency, and her tuning gear had wavered, unable to lock on.

"What are you going to do next," I said.

She shifted slightly in her chair. Both of us had forgotten to fetch coffees. She craned her neck around to look behind her at the noisy espresso bar, then at me, then back into that mysterious dimension on the tabletop.

"I offered to go out to Reims for a day, if he would meet me there," she said. "Alain said to wait and see what his schedule would be. He's going to call," she added rapidly, with that peculiar admixture in her voice of sudden bravado, reassurance, and trailing-off. Listening to Rita had the effect of making me begin to feel vague and uncertain, as if perhaps I had imagined much of my own personal history; as if we were both fading systematically into the noisy air. I squared myself and sat up taller, leaning toward her a little to stretch my spine.

"Rita, what do want from this?" I said it quietly.

She looked at the table. Her eyes had dulled some, yet her voice kept the careful modulations of a coffee shop hostess.

"I want to tell him that he doesn't have to worry if he just wants to be friends. I mean he's so nice and all, and…I would be very happy just to be friends with him and…respect him as a friend, and…maybe we can still keep something up after I have to go back to the states ..." She looked at me.

"That's what you want me to write in French for you?"

She nodded, coloring in mottled patches. "I just can't say it right," she said, "and I can never think fast enough to say it when I'm with him." She didn't have Alain's address, but she could hand the letter to him when they next met. Rita had tried to improve her French during classes. She had even hired a private tutor recommended by Madame, a plump woman who also worked at the dorm's switchboard. They would sit opposite each other here in the coffee bar, and Rita would écouter and répéter until her head rang and throbbed.

She frowned.

"I thought I would try to stay in France. If I could get a job in Epernay near Reims, where the champagne cellars are…I'm going to start asking around, you know?" Her eyes fixed suddenly on mine. She seemed to hope I would finish her sentences for her, and in doing so, shoehorn her into these designs. Again I was repelled. Was it that Rita somehow embodied, at forty-six, what the rest of us work so hard to contain, or stave off, or simply deny? It was nearly unbearable to watch her—cut free and floating, tumbling and dying in deep space. My skin itched. But I heard myself urging Rita on in her ballooning, dream-cloud notions, telling her there was no reason why she should not branch out, check around, see what was available—every cliche that might appease, that might help ease me away. She listened with that air she had of hearing something else at the same time; something hard to make out. I squeezed her shoulder as I rose from the table, and almost in penance for racing away—like putting my hasty signature to a bill—agreed we should have dinner soon.

That evening, I sat down at the formica desk. Beneath the whey-thin fluorescent light, I wrote in French: *Dear Alain. You have been so kind, it is hard for me to tell you directly how glad I am to know you, so I'll try to explain it in writing. Good feelings between people can take many forms. Please understand that I will be quite content if we can remain friends, and I look forward to our continuing friendship. Thank you for everything.* I hope you will accept my sincerest best wishes. I posted this in Rita's mail slot. The following day in my own mail, I found a small chocolate bar called Yes, and a tiny bottle of lily-scented oil. Her note, in that deliberate, round hand, said merci mille fois. A thousand thanks.

As the semester neared its close, the weather never got any better. Every day I cranked open the wooden-slatted awning—to find the same lead sky and freezing rain. I had become immersed in the usual last-minute crises of my students, with final exams, faculty convenings—all the detritus that teachers mock and at the same time, to which they devote themselves with a kind of annoyed urgency; organizing their lives to attend and fulfill.

Amid those weeks I often walked a few blocks after dinner, allowing the cold to clear my head for the evening's stack of reading; one night as I rounded the corner at St. Jacques and rue de la Santé I saw Rita through the brasserie window. She was sitting alone with a glass of red wine, a small brown ceramic carafe beside that, and—to my astonishment—a cigarette in one dangling hand. She looked at no one. She did not look well. I dreaded contact with her and, despising myself, hurried past the window. At about 11:30 that night I was wakened by the old-fashioned shriek of the dorm telephone.

"I need your opinion," she said.

"Can it wait until morning?" I wondered.

"Please."

I dressed, and went downstairs to find Rita waiting in the lobby. She wore a rumpled fuchsia sweat suit; her hair was a bit matted on one side. She smiled briefly, but her eyes seemed wild.

"Let's walk," I said. We pushed open the big glass doors and stepped into the dark chill. It still smelled of rush-hour exhaust. Students were hanging from the waist out the dorm windows above us, splashing beer, waving and hooting at each other. We walked toward Alesia, the middle-class neighborhoods lined with apartment buildings, many of their lights still on, though it was a Sunday night and they would be herding their toddlers to school in a matter of hours. Rita did not glance up at the apartment windows as I did, but studied their dull reflection in the damp pavement as she walked, and spoke.

Rita and Alain had had another date at Vincennes. During which they had ridden in a little mock train car around the Parc Floral, eaten ice creams, and had several photos of themselves snapped by someone with a Polaroid; Rita clutched the pictures like pressed flowers as they walked along the cold banks of the manmade pond. Alain had told Rita he cared deeply for her and wanted no harm to come to her, and Rita had finally been unable to contain her yearning: she had asked Alain why she could not come to visit him where he lived. Alain had again blamed his bizarre conductor schedule, and the fact that the loaned apartment had no phone. C'est pas la peine, he assured her. Don't worry about it. It's too much hassle. He put his arms around her and kissed her. He would call her.

Three weeks passed, and Rita decided, toward the end of that time, to get her French tutor's help looking for Alain's name on Minitel, the French computer Internet directory. Rita told her tutor she was trying to locate an old friend. After some effort poring through the columns on the printout, the two women found "A. Lemieux" among the Reims listings. It was the only one in Reims.

We were passing the black glass of the patisserie windows, Parc Montsouris and the university. Occasionally an indistinct figure would approach and silently pass, yanked along by a sniffing dog on its leash.

"What did you do?" I prompted her after a moment.
"I Phoned the listed number," she said simply
"And?" "disgusted with my own eagerness
"A young woman's voice," Rita said after a moment
"How young?"
"Girlfriend young. Wife young." And Rita's drawl was slow and entirely astonished, the way it had been when she had told about stepping onto the wrong train. As if trying to state the case in a way that made sense, like an equation. Call a number, hear a woman.

The third secret, I thought.

"And then?" I urged her on. I wanted to hear the sound of the man frying like an electrocuted bug. I felt a sort of furtive, angry glee, like someone who could not stop licking stale icing from a cake.

Rita had hung up. Then she had gathered the Polaroid snapshots of herself and Alain at the park, and written an intimate note as best she could, in French. Cher Alain, remember these, I hope they please you, until next time, with all my love. She had carefully wrapped the note around the Polaroids and mailed them to the address given for A. Lemieux in the Minitel listings for Reims.

I said nothing for a minute. Then I said, "Let's head back."

I glanced at her as we walked, but Rita never looked up from studying the sidewalk. I could see my breath, and hers. The cold was seeping through my thin leather soles; my toes were numbing. We didn't speak again until we reached the dorm and sat in the empty, fluorescent lobby, perched on the edge of the abstract metallic seats by the big coffee table, like a couple of talk-show types. I asked her to tell me the rest.

She looked at her lap, at her clasped hand. Two days later, Rita told me, Alain called. She had asked him whether he had yet received something in the mail.

His voice had grown stiff, and wary. No. Why, he had asked.

Rita told him the Minitel story,

Alain, she said, had become frantic on the phone "C'été pas moi, Rita! C'été pas moi! C'est pas juste; tu n'as pas le droit!" It wasn't me! It's not fair! You've no right! And he had hung up on her.

Rita looked at me in mild wonder, like a child waiting to be told about the moon's pull upon the tides.

"Yes," I suddenly said. "Yes. It was exactly what you should have done. The son of a bitch conniving bastard." My own language startled me yet did not supply the punch I craved.

She smiled wanly. "I'll go to bed now," she said

I took her hands.

"Rita. Semester's almost finished," I said. "You'll be fine. You'll be out of here soon."

I watched her walk to the elevator and give a little nod before she entered.

I didn't hear from Rita thereafter, or see her again, until the last day of the program.

The cold had, in final days, given way to muggy heat, though the sky was still the color of silt. I was packed and waiting in the lobby, with my luggage, for the taxi to Charles de Gaulle. Though it wasn't a full-fledged graduation, it had all the queer earmarks—an odd and giddying weightlessness, the sense of roles and hierarchies erasing, of imminent free fall. A bus for the students was already rumbling outside; they were stopping in excited little huddles to exchange addresses and embrace and swear to keep in close touch. The young women were triumphant, perfumed and rouged for the plane flight, during which they planned, they said, to take over the aircraft for "a big trans-Atlantic party." Some of them had found their temporary French boyfriends; those less certain had pretended to; the shyest and plainest had taken refuge in furious all-night group journal-writing sessions, or in going to pray at Sacre Coeur.

Beyond the milling students I saw Rita slip through the dorm's glass doors. She was carefully groomed, in black sweater, slacks, and a brown suede jacket. Her blue eyes bulged under fresh makeup, carefully applied. Her hair had just been brushed out from the hot-curler set. I stood to signal her. "Here!" She raised her eyebrows, and walked to me in that carefully placed gait—what was it like?—like someone practicing to walk, balancing a book on her head for finishing school. Practicing in the waiting room of the life she hoped to lead.

I sat her down. The noise from the crowd of students was rico-

The Waiting Room

cheting through the big room; I had to yell to ask Rita her plans. Rita was not leaving Paris, it seemed. She had heard again from Alain. He had phoned.

I gaped at her. "What are you saying. What are you telling me?"

Rita smiled, a mysterious twitching at the corners of her mouth. She said Alain told her he wanted to see her once more. She had decided already, she said, to try to stay in Paris anyway, try to find a job in the champagne country, and now, also so she could see him. But first she would look for an apartment here in Paris, she said, to figure things out. She had just a little money left, and she thought she would try to set something up here with it. What did I think? She searched my face. Did I think that was all right?

"Rita." I looked at her, and had to boom my voice to make myself heard above the shrilling kids. "If you have any money left at all, you need it to get a foothold back home."

"It might be something completely reasonable, something I can understand." she yelled back, and she colored, and the corners of her mouth twitched. I realized she was talking past me, about Alain's chicanery. And then I grasped it: Soyons raisonnable. Tu peaux me comprende. She was quoting his words. Rita had skipped a chapter in today's report. She had already met with Alain since his call; he had persuaded her of some shabby nonsense; she had slept with him. Because anything was better than waiting in the waiting room. Anything, anything at all, was better than that. I saw my taxi pull up in front of the dorm and I rose to slice my way through the screaming twenty-year-olds. I took a step back from her. Turning to flag the cab driver. Rita's hand went to my arm. "It might be just the right direction . . . I can keep up my French,": she was shouting. "Don't you agree, Emily? Don't you think?": And blanketed by the din, her voice trailed off, in familiar, imploring, quavering, watery hope.

Paris

Ellen Gilchrist

A young man is dead and maybe we could have stopped it. That's what I wake up with every morning. Until a month ago I was a completely happy person. Who knows, maybe I'll be happy again.

Reality expands exponentially. It meets itself coming and going. It is a net, a web; touch one strand and the whole thing quivers. Get caught and you cannot get away. Sticky stuff, reality. Spiders understand this metaphor. It had nothing to do with me. I say this over and over again, like a mantra.

There was no reason why I shouldn't go to Paris. My young friend, Tannin, was writing a book about me. He needed me to inspire him and give him material. I don't think he knew he was writing about me. He thought he was writing a book about three girls in Paris living in an apartment and talking all the time about their lovers. Only all three sounded like me, my hysteria, how I make every utterance an oath or a promise. I can't help it. I was poisoned in the womb. If you don't buy first causes, don't read on.

I'm a journalist and a writer of novels. My name is Rhoda Manning and I'm fifty-eight years old and you'd never believe that either. People who believe in fairies don't age.

So on the fifth of May I climbed into the belly of the whale and crossed the Atlantic Ocean and arrived at Orly about seven in the morning. Tannin met me at the plane. His fifty-eight-year-old muse in a wrinkled white linen suit and two-inch spectator pumps getting bravely off a plane with her hair cut short for the mission. I used to have lovers his age. Now I only want the good part, the youthful energy, the sheer delight. Coming out to Orly at seven in the morning to squire me through customs. The ones I had for lovers might have done that. But none of them spoke flawless Parisian French.

There are many love affairs in the world, more ways to love, Horatio, than you dream of. I had been practicing all my life for this. Having brothers, raising sons, loving young men. And now, in my Senior Citizenship, Tannin had been delivered to me. To love, to understand, to nourish, to adore. He had written me a letter to say he liked a book I wrote. It was a book about a friend who died an early death. I will write about you, I had told the friend. I will not let you die. Do it, he had answered. If you write it from the heart, it will be good. I had and it was and I was as proud of it as anything I had ever written.

Also, it gave Tannin to me. The book had come to him from the Book-of-the-Month Club and he forgot to send it back. So he read it and then he wrote to me and told me he wanted to be a writer. I throw such letters away every day. This one was different. It had a lilt, a ring, it made me laugh. He asked my advice about writing schools and I told him to come up here. That Randolph was a genius and would not harm him. Randolph is the director of the writing program.

So Tannin came to Fayetteville and became my friend and the next thing I knew I was flying to Paris to "hang out with him" while he wrote his book.

He called me frantically two days before I left to say he had a visitor, a young man who had gone to Sewanee with him. "He's driving me crazy," he said. "He's in a terrible mood. He hates everything in Paris. I took him to hear Ravel at the Sorbonne. He hated Ravel. I hope he'll be gone by the time you get here, but he might not be. I'm really sorry. He just showed up. I invited him a year ago. I never dreamed he'd come."

"Maybe he's disoriented. That happened to me once, in Heidelberg. I just got completely disoriented. I had to go home."

"I don't know what's wrong with him. He quit his job a month ago. Maybe that's it. He was working for his dad in Nashville."

"Don't worry about it. Nothing will stop us from having fun in Paris. Did you get tickets to the ballet?"
"Yes. They're supposed to be good seats. They'd better be."
"My cousin plays in the orchestra. We'll meet her after the performance. I haven't seen her since she was in high school."
"Good. That's fine. We'll do anything you want to do. I'm so glad you're coming."

As soon as we collected my bags we went to my hotel and sat in the café drinking coffee and talking. We hadn't seen each other in four weeks but it seemed a year. Our sagas engage us. His are as real to me as mine. "So what's the friend's name?" I asked. "And is he better?"
"His name is William and he's worse. Now he has a cold. He's asleep in my room. He's going to the ballet with us tomorrow night."
"That's fine. I want to meet him. Don't worry, Tannin. Nothing is wrong. I'm elated to be here. Look at this weather. This is paradise. My plan is to stay awake all afternoon and take a sleeping pill and crash about six and sleep till dawn. How does that sound to you?"
"Fantastic. Should you be drinking coffee?"
"It won't matter. I have a Xanax. It will knock me out." We giggle. We laughed as if that were the funniest thing in the world, as if it were deeply, wildly, madly, hysterically funny.

We left the hotel and walked up the rue de Montalembert to the boulevard St-Germain and followed it to the Seine. We stood on the bridge and watched people and talked about the swimming pool that had sunk in the river the night before.
"A floating swimming pool that's been here since the forties. Think what would have happened if it had been in the daytime. If people had been there. I wish I could have seen it sink."
"So do I. What a phenomenon. A huge floating swimming pool sinking into the Seine. *Mon dieu!*" We laughed again. It was incredibly, divinely, hilariously funny. No one ever gets that tickled when they are alone. Only two people can know something is that funny.

"In sight of Notre Dame Cathedral. This may be a sign. Listen, I told William I'd meet him for lunch. I never thought you'd want to stay awake. We don't have to go. I could go by there and tell him I'm not coming."

"I want to. Come on. I want to go. I really do. Why are you so worried about my meeting William?"

"Because it's your vacation. You shouldn't have to baby-sit my friends."

"I want to meet him." I took his arm and we walked along the river to the Jardin des Tuileries and across the gardens to the Café du Palais Royale, a bright café with pots of orange flowers and brilliant paintings on the walls. We found a table and sat down and began to read the menu. A young man came hurrying toward us through the tables. He had curly blond hair and blue eyes and looked enough like Tannin to be his twin. "William Watkins Weckter," Tannin said. "The fourth or fifth. My old roommate at Sewanee. He's dying to meet you."

"I read your books," he said. "I used to talk about them all the time."

"Oh, my. Sit down. Are you feeling better? Tannin said you had been sick."

"It's nothing. A summer cold. Well, I quit my job last month. I'm out on the street. That should give you a cold, don't you think?" He laughed and took a handkerchief out of his pocket and stood up and went outside and blew his nose. When he came back in he picked up the conversation and went right on. He didn't seem depressed to me. Just at loose ends, like half the young people I meet. No children, no responsibilities they can't leave. They are free, in the deepest and most terrible sense of the word. Cut loose, dismounted, disengaged. Not Tannin though, he's in love with the muse, the sight of his words upon the page. Artists are the same in any age, always lost and always found.

So here was William with a degree in history and a minor in biology and nothing to do. He had worked for his father in an office supply store in Nashville for a while, now he was wandering around the world. "I better see it while I can," he said. "When I go back to work I won't have a vacation for a year."

"The age of commerce may be over," I said. "I've been thinking of this. It's time for live theater, beautiful buildings, parks. There must be things for young people to do that will engage them in their brightest minds. It's this transition that is painful. Find out what you will to do and do it. What do you want to do, William? Do you have any idea?"

"Something worth keeping. Something I could talk about. When I was young I liked to keep records. I wrote down what I did each day." He looked off into the gardens outside the café. We finished our coffee. William insisted on paying for our lunch. Nothing would dissuade him. Then he left us, and Tannin and I walked back to my hotel. There were young people dressed in costumes from the seventeenth century wandering around the Tuileries looking beautiful and mysterious. They weren't selling anything. We couldn't figure out why they were there.

"Gratuitous beauty," Tannin declared. "France. I am happiest when I am here. It's my mother's fault. She did this to me."

"I'm fading," I answered. "Take me to my bed. I'll see you in the morning."

Tannin delivered me to my hotel and I went upstairs and unpacked and ordered some Evian and drank half a bottle of it with a Xanax and went to sleep with the windows open. I was on the seventh floor of the Hôtel Montalembert, where Buckminster Fuller used to stay with his entourage. Outside my window I could see the Eiffel Tower and the streets leading to the river and les Champs Elysées. I slept. Like a lamb in a meadow I slept away the hours until dawn.

I woke in Paris. I stretched out my muscles in the bed. Pulled the beautiful pillows into my arms. Goose down, from some lovely flock of geese somewhere in the land of France. This elegant old culture. I lay in bed and looked around the room. It was black and white. White walls, black painted furniture, a soft design of the chairs. Another bolder print on the bedcover. White linen drapes pulled back from dormer windows. I won't do a thing I don't want to do, I decided. I will not hurry. I curled back into a ball and daydreamed for a while, imagining the ballet we would see that evening. The Paris Opéra House with its ceiling painted by Chagall.

Ballets by Balanchine and Robbins. I had not seen ballet in fourteen months. I was badly overdue for a ballet.

I rose from the bed and walked over to the window and stood leaning out the casement in my white silk nightgown. When I'm at home I sleep in flannel. See what this city does for me. I drank the rest of the Evian and dressed in a black pantsuit and went down to the café for petit déjeuner. A waiter brought me the *Herald Tribune* and I read Russell Baker's column and drank the best coffee in the world and ate a brioche and raspberries from the Dordogne. I was getting more civilized every minute. I was almost urbane. The city and the day stretched out before me. I thought of Tannin, not ten blocks away in his room overlooking the Luxembourg Gardens. I thought of William, with his upper-respiratory infection and his pretty face. I thought of my young cousin playing her violin at the Paris Opéra. I thought of Chagall and the light coming in the glass windows onto my table and the perfect weather and how lucky I was to live in such a world.

I went upstairs and changed into street shoes and left the hotel and walked for an hour, exploring side streets, stopping at a salon to make an appointment for my hair, windowshopping.

When I got back to the hotel there were messages. Tannin was coming to take me to lunch. My cousin was home and would I call her. It made me giddy, to be in a city this beautiful, in cool weather, with young people to talk to, and nothing, not a single thing going wrong, and no longer in boyfriend jail. I was not in love with anyone and I did not want to be. BOND NO MORE, it said on notes I had scattered around my house. I had written it and I meant it. I was free to let the whole world be my lover.

Free at last from the obsessive weight of love affairs. Free from waiting around a hotel room for a husband or a lover to decide what I could or could not do. Free from men turning on television sets.

I combed my hair, put on my two-inch heels, went down to the lobby and Tannin was there, smiling and embracing me, as excited as I was. We left the hotel and walked until we found a sidewalk café that we liked and sat in the shade of a plane tree giggling and talking and telling stories and watching everything. There is nothing on earth like friendship. It is God's love, God's ambrosia, the one thing we never have to pay for or regret.

"That man is looking at you." Tannin laughed. "Men have been checking you out all morning."

"It's the damnedest thing. I mean, *mon dieux*, the minute you stop being available, men start wanting you. They can smell it a mile away. It has nothing to do with age or beauty."

"It's true. If we think we can't have it, it becomes interesting to us."

"You can't manufacture it. You have to really be out of the game. I am. You can't imagine how much I do not want to have another affair of any kind."

"Look at that, Rhoda. Over in the corner." I glanced at the couple kissing in the corner. A middle-aged man and a woman in a low-cut blouse. They looked like some inferior breed of human, the expression on their faces was completely infantile.

"Do you think they just did it or are they just about to go somewhere and do it?"

"Probably both." A waiter approached the couple and set a huge glass of ice cream with whipped cream and cherries and chocolate sauce down in front of the woman. The man picked up a spoon and began to feed her. Tannin touched my arm. We shook with laughter. We almost fell off our chairs. We could not contain ourselves. We paid the bill and walked off down the street and found a building to lean against and laughed until we cried.

I slept in the late afternoon and dressed and met Tannin and William in the lobby and we set out for the opera house. "I've never seen a ballet," William said. "Is it okay to admit that?"

"I was older than you before I saw one that was good," I answered. "This is the World Series you're going to see. Except for Maurice Bejart and the Ballet of the Twentieth Century. That's the best to me, the nonpareil."

Later, after the first ballet, which was the Balanchine, he said, "Don't the ones in the chorus mind? They never get to be the star?"

"Prima ballerinas," I told him. "Listen, these are great athletes. They don't mind someone being the prima ballerina any more than a football team minds having a great running back. They have a wonderful life. They live to dance, to be up there on that stage, with that music, doing this for us. Dancers never grow old. I wish I could have been one."

"Well," I grudgingly admitted, later, in the lobby, at intermission, with a glass of wine. "They ruin their feet. They tear up their toes. What they're doing is unnatural, but that's why it's so hard and why the excitement of it never dies."

We went back to our seats, which were in a box to the left of the stage. Above our heads, the divine ceiling by Chagall. The curtains opened. Two dancers came on stage. Behind them were the flats which had also been painted by Chagall. *Entree et pas-de-deux.* Magic. *Danse des garçons* with tables covered by umbrellas. More magic. Then the *danse des filles*, with small umbrellas everywhere. It was the dance of the day we had just spent in Paris, with the burden of weight dissolved in color. The human spirit turned loose to fly, transcend itself. This ballet alone would have been worth the trip across the ocean.

I had arranged for us to meet my cousin after the performance. May Chatevin Debardeleben. Her name was almost whispered in my family. She's in Paris, they would say. She plays the violin for the Paris ballet.

She was just as I remembered her, a blithe young girl with long dusty blond hair and violet eyes. Even as a child she had carried herself with dignity and grace. It had not surprised me when I heard she had flown the coop, escaped the massive tentacles of our family.

We found her in the orchestra pit, holding her violin against her black taffeta dress. I introduced everyone, embraced her, and begged her to come to dinner with us. "All right," she said. "Let me put this violin away. I won't bother to change to street clothes, if you don't mind." She was so absolutely southern, the same young girl from Abbeville, Louisiana, where her mother played the organ at the Episcopal Church.

While she put the violin in the case I squeezed Tannin's hand. I was so proud of my lovely young cousin. All this time William had not spoken. Now, when May Chatevin snapped the clasps on the case, he reached out a hand and took it from her. "I played a violin when I was a kid," he said. "But I had to stop."

"Oh, why was that?" She was wearing large hornrimmed glasses. She reached up and took them off as she waited for his answer.

"Because it interfered with baseball practice. Then I broke a finger and it was in a cast for a year."

"That's terrible." She moved near him. "That's the worst thing I ever heard."

"I used to love the way it fit into the case."

"You could start again. It's not too late."

"You think so?"

"Sure. There are wonderful teachers here. Do you speak French?"

"I won't be here long."

"Let's start walking," Tannin said. "You can't solve this on an empty stomach."

We had dinner at a brasserie along the Seine. The lights from the barges going along the river climbed the trunks of the trees, then filled the crowns, then climbed back down. Afterward, an afterglow. A heavy metaphor for love, if anyone needed one in Paris.

May Chatevin and William were in love before we ever got to the brasserie. They had paired up as soon as we left the opera house. They walked behind us, their heads bent toward one another. I had forgotten how fast it happens, had forgotten young men's bodies, the cold shaking power of desire, had been glad to forget it, as I now had other things to do, being in the universe on this clearer, older plane.

"My guardian angel must have finally made it across the ocean," William was saying across the table. "Everyone who goes to Sewanee gets a guardian angel. When we go onto the campus we check him at the gates. When we leave we pick him up again. We don't need him at Sewanee, you see, as it's the closest place to heaven." William laughed out loud. He was laughing at everything. And his cold had disappeared. It was the truth, what I told his parents later. He was the happiest young man I'd ever seen. In contrast to Tannin, who is as hysterical as I am. Searching, searching, dreaming, playing out the string. Philip Larkin has a metaphor for this. People sitting on the cliffs waiting for a white-sailed armada of hopes to come in. They arrive, Larkin says, but they never anchor. "Only one ship is seeking us," the poem ends. "A black-sailed unfamiliar, towing at its back a huge and breathless silence. In its wake, no waters breed or break."

The four of us became inseparable. We went to the Sorbonne to hear a string quartet play Brahms. We walked in the Tuileries and had lunch at Les Deux Magots. We strolled the boulevard St-Germain and went to Sulka to look at the ties. We walked along the Seine and saw the small blue asters in the flower shops and I told the story of V. K. Ratcliff's trip to New York City to the wedding of Eula Varner Snopes to the Jewish Communist and how V. K. bought a tie the color of asters and how the Russian woman kissed him on the mouth as she tied it around his neck.

We talked of writing and painting and music. We harvested the beauty of the city and fed it to each other. One day we rented a car and I drove to Dieppe to see the coast. On the way home the skies were full of clouds and over a field of young corn we watched three parachuters playing with the wind. We talked of books we had read and artists we admired. We went to the Rodin museum and stood in line for fifty minutes. "Rilke came here every afternoon," Tannin said. "He adored Rodin. '*Rodin, c'est lui qui a inspiré le poete*,' Ran Rilke."

"I want to buy the tickets," I said. "Tell me what to say?"

"*Quatre. S'il vous plaît.*"

"*Quatre. S'il vous plaît,*" I told the lady in the cage and counted out the money as if I were six years old.

The *billets* were beautiful, reproductions of the statue called *Le Bourgeois de Calais*, 1895. Musée Rodin, 77 rue de Varenne, Paris.

We had an audience with the brilliant translator, Barbara Bray, and took her to a concert with us at a cathedral. May Chatevin and I had our hair done at Julien et Claude, Haute Coiffure, St-Germain-des-Près. We stood outside the Louvre and watched the tourists going in. We bought a disposable camera and took photographs of each other by the statues of the continents. We went to Chanel and saw Catherine Deneuve shopping for costumes for a movie. We pretended not to know who she was and looked the other way.

Often, in the afternoons, May Chatevin and William would disappear until suppertime. Tannin had sworn off women until his book was finished. And I had found out a wonderful thing. You do not have to be getting laid to be ecstatic in this city which worships love.

Often while they were gone we went somewhere and wrote in our notebooks. He needed a château for a love scene in his book and we found one in the country and went there several times to draw it in our minds.

"William's sister is calling him twice a day," Tannin told me. "His family's furious. They want him to come home."

"His sister?"

"She's visiting Rome with her husband. She wants him to come there and go home with them."

"What does he tell them?"

"He tells them no. He says he's in love with a girl from the States."

"What's going on?" I asked my cousin, when I had her alone one afternoon.

"I'm in love with him. I want him to stay here with me."

"How could he work? An American can't get work in Paris."

"It's a problem." She looked right at me. The old fierceness, selfishness, call it what you will. In the last two generations our family has a divorce rate about twice the national average. The reason is that look. This arrogance we breed or foster, here it was again, in Paris, in this twenty-nine-year-old girl with her perfect ear and talented hands. "I'm writing a symphony. The Saint Louis Symphony is going to perform it when it's done. I can't leave now. This city is my muse. I have to stay another year or two."

"Then what will happen?"

"I don't know. I want him to stay. He can live with me. He knows that. He can get a visa."

"What would he do for money?"

"I don't know. Maybe we have to live today and not think about it." I had been wrong. She had stopped being southern. She stood beside the window in my room, looking out onto the roofs of Paris. She was where she had meant to go, she was where she meant to be.

I changed my plane reservation. I decided to stay another week. One morning Tannin met me in the hotel café for breakfast.

"He's leaving at noon," Tannin said. "He's run out of money and his sister won't leave him alone. He's going to Rome and fly home with them in his brother-in-law's plane. His family has lots of money, but they won't give it to him."

"They shouldn't. That's good. That's right."

"He's in love with your cousin. That's our fault, Rhoda. We did that, you and I. He's really broken up about leaving. Do you think she loves him?"

"She loves her work. She's writing a symphony. She wrote one last year that was played by the New Orleans Symphony Orchestra. She has an agreement to write one for Saint Louis. She's going to be a star. Yes, I think she loves him. She wants to keep him here for a pet."

"He came home early last night. I guess they had a fight."

"It's not our fault, Tannin. That's nuts to think that."

We left the café. We walked to the Champs Elysees and window-shopped. We went to the Luxembourg Gardens and rode the carousel. We bought beignets with powdered sugar and sat upon a bench and ate them with our fingers.

"I'd better call May Chatevin when I get home," I said. "She has to play tonight. Maybe we can meet her later and get some supper."

"It's not our fault, Rhoda, remember that."

"I know. It isn't. By God, it has nothing to do with us. We didn't do it."

Neither was it our fault that the Italian Mafia chose that day to load up a car with plastic explosives and drive it into the train station to Firenze just as William got off the train. For what? To turn around and come back to Paris? To buy a package of cigarettes? To call May Chatevin?

    I don't buy group guilt. Or any of that politically correct bullshit. Most of the people in the world are doing the best they can with whatever knowledge they have managed to attain or been fed by whatever myths they were raised under. So, somewhere in the darkness of the underside of existence in the ancient land of Italy, someone, or two or three benighted souls, stuffed a Fiat full of explosives smuggled in from God knows where and with or without a driver ran it into the side of the old section of the Firenze train station where maybe William had just disembarked long enough to buy a sandwich or a drink or a newspaper. He was trying to learn Italian, he had said one night when we were sitting beside the Seine using all our pidgin languages. Tannin is the only one of us who has mastered anything other than English, although May Chatevin's French is charming and she gets by.

    Tannin and May Chatevin and I were together that night. We left my hotel about six and walked to the Jardin des Plantes to see the menagerie. It was cool that evening and May Chatevin was wearing pale yellow silk pants and a green silk jacket. Her hair was pulled back into a chignon. I thought she looked like her mother that night, as she was sad and trying to hide the sadness. "I couldn't leave now," she said a dozen times. "I couldn't just leave all this and go back home. I think he understood that. Did he say anything to you, Tannin? What did he say?"

    "That he is in love with you, of course. He doesn't know what he's going to do. Maybe go to work for his brother-in-law. Make some money and come back for you."

    "You could go and visit him," I put in. "Surely you don't have to work incessantly."

    "Until I finish the symphony I can't take a day away from it. I've wasted two weeks as it is, but not entirely. I've been working in the mornings." We were walking along the rue Claude Bernard, trying to find our way to the boulevard de Vaugirard, where there was a Brazilian restaurant Tannin knew about.

    After dinner we decided to see the late showing of *Much Ado About Nothing* in English with French subtitles. It was over about eleven fifteen and the two young people left me at my hotel and Tannin walked May Chatevin home. He is struggling with his novel and takes every opportunity to put off going home to write it, which he does in the middle of the night no matter how much I lecture him on the efficacy of the morning hours.

I went up to my room and turned on the television set for the first time since I'd been in Paris. I turned on CNN and settled back into the pillows with a glass of Evian. It was the first event on the news. The train station in flames, people running with their hands up in the air, firemen spraying the flames with chemicals, demolished automobiles parked outside the station.

I watched the full report. Then I called Tannin. He returned to my hotel and came up to my room and we began to call crazily around three countries trying to find something out.

"Let's go down there," I said. "Rent a car."

"We have to stay here. He might have my address with him if he was hurt. He might call."

"What about May Chatevin?"

"Wait until morning. If she knew she would have called. What could she do this time of night?"

"It wouldn't be him. He wouldn't die. He's not the type."

"Anyone can die, Rhoda. Anytime. Anywhere."

"Thinking he was a failure?"

"He didn't think that. He just couldn't decide what to do."

"We're overreacting. I shouldn't have called you. You should be at home doing your work."

"Do you think he was in it?"

"I don't know."

"Neither do I."

Tannin slept on the sofa in my room. We woke up early and dressed and went to May Chatevin's apartment. She had read it in the paper. "If he wasn't hurt, he would have called us," she kept saying. "He said he'd call when he got there."

"We can't be sure."

"Then why hasn't he called?"

"What's his sister's name?"

Paris

"I don't know."
"Should we call his parents in the States?"
"No. Oh, God, no. What if he's all right?"

In the end Tannin and May Chatevin had a car delivered and started driving. I stayed by the phone. They stopped and called every two hours. In between the second and third call the American embassy called to say his name was on the list of the dead.

THE LIST OF THE DEAD. In June, in a peaceful Europe, the summer he was twenty-five. Random, inexplicable.

I told her when she called at three that afternoon. They went on to Firenze to see if they could claim the body. I asked the embassy to get me his parents' phone number. I sat in zazen on the floor of my room and waited for the courage to make the call. I could have looked out the window and seen the Eiffel Tower if I wanted to.

I got his father on the phone. I told him his son had been completely happy when he left for Rome. I told him his son had been the happiest man I had ever known. I asked if I could meet the daughter in Firenze. If I could do anything at all for them. I gave them my phone number in the United States. I said they could come to visit me and I would tell them about every minute of the weeks gone by. "He was the happiest young man I've ever known," I told them. "What fine parents you must have been. What a delightful son you had." Had. Here in the maya of space and time. On the planet Earth, in nineteen hundred and ninety-three A.D., in the only world there is.

*   *   *

Two days later Tannin and May Chatevin got back to Paris. They had met the sister. Tannin had helped identify the body. May Chatevin had lost ten pounds. I put her to bed in her apartment with one of my three remaining Xanax tablets. I sat in her living room while she slept and tried to read *Le Monde*. Tannin had gone home to rest.

"Get up tomorrow morning and write," I told him. "Now will you believe? Now will you go on and write your hero's death?"

"No," he answered. "I'm going to skip over to the part that takes place in the United States. After the child is born."

"Requiem. Yes, go on."

"We got a dog the last year we were at Sewanee. This brown dog we found at the pound. We had to hide it from the landlord."

"What happened to it?"

"He took it to Nashville and gave it to his mother. I guess she's still got it. He used to let it ride in the car with him everywhere he went. That dog loved to ride in automobiles. He'd put his paws up on the window and stick his head out. Everyone knew our dog. We called it Vain for a girl friend he once had."

"I told his father he was the happiest man I had ever known."

"He might have been. Now he is. Now he doesn't care." We had been whispering. Now we embraced. He left me there. I opened French *Vogue* and began to read an article about how to dye the hair on my legs. We don't really need hair on our bodies anymore. But nature keeps it there in case things change.

Lightning North of Paris

MARK HELPRIN

It was approaching five o'clock on a cool afternoon in late October. Harry Spence sat on a stone railing in front of the Jeu de Paume, and as he waited for Shannon he looked through a maze of autumn trees stirred by a wind promising of winter and challenging in its direct cold northernness, a wind which lighted fires. Shannon was extremely tall and graceful. This, her face, and her dancer's body were a continual proclamation that she be taken dead seriously. In fact, anyone not always alert with her would find himself left behind as if in the slipstream of a fast train which had just passed. She stared other women down like a man; they often hated her. In a café she had the same effect as music or a fireplace, quickly becoming the center. Men were drawn to her because they did not immediately fall in love. Her power put them off until they got close enough and then went mad, leaving lovely wives and waiting for Shannon on the street, where if she passed they became speechless as she crossed in leotards and a long skirt, a soft silk scarf trailing.

When Harry took up with Shannon he knew she would leave, but he was privileged to be with her for a time because he would not scare. He was always on guard, convincing her that he too was arbitrary and painfully free, as independent as a cloud sailing across frontiers. It was an act he put on successfully, but it was exhausting. Only a young man could have kept it up. He thought that if her demands had been made on a man older than twenty-five he would have died; frequency of intercourse was only a small part of the monumental task. That year was like a Channel swim. He wondered how he had done it, and how Shannon could always remain Shannon. They all moved like figures inside a furnace, which at the time was appropriate, and constructive, for they sat during the night at small desks and penned words or music, or played instruments, or painted, not knowing who was really good and who would fall back to the small towns of New York and Ohio never to be heard from again, perhaps to be unknown interpreters of those who had remained.

Harry Spence had not come to Paris because it was Paris, although once there he realized that even in imitation long after the originals (none of whom had really been first) the city was still a blaze and a dream. He had been granted a restricted fellowship stipulating that he live in a section of Paris dear to the benefactor and considered by him to be magical in its effect on musical composition. When flying into the city that September, he wished he were a writer of words rather than music. The prospect was stunning, spread white into the bordering fields. Masculine ministries enclosed luxurious gardens of mathematical green—from the air this appeared to be the hallmark of the city. He had the feeling that he was returning to the vortex of civilization, having indeed been there before, that the inhabitants were possessed of a strange combination of clarity and feeling and were at that moment lighting fires over secret magnetic zones which crisscrossed the earth, making artists, and converged at Paris in the center of wheat and wine-filled French prairies sobered and chilled by blasts from the North.

Wherever children gather at a forge or fire, its red heat giving them warmth in darkness, they learn quickly principles of art. This is what Harry had thought when very young as he sat by a fire with his father and uncle and grandfather in the middle of violet autumn fields which they knew would see frost by morning. The grandfather had passed through Paris on his way to the front; the father and uncle had crossed the Seine riding on the same tank. They had ached from their hearts to see Paris in peace, to live and work there. They had carried cartridges through Saint-Germain-des-Prés and been continually on edge and nervous, for they then were sent to bosky woods near the German border to fight and kill. After his father returned, his life had calmed. He never yearned for war, but he knew it had made him. There was plenty of thunder in the following peace, haystack-leveling winds to test him, obstacles to his dreams, but none of this later adversity had defined and shaped him as had the war. He wished with all his might that he would not communicate this to his son, that the boy, born after the fighting, would find other means to know himself and would not repeat the horror for the sake of becoming a man. He wished for his son peaceful storms and not the waxen white light of artillery duels. He prayed for this. And Harry was different, soft, a baby beyond his time, unknowing of combat and the continual deathly backdrop of war, an almost effeminate university-bred tortoise-shell-glassed composer of music. His father and uncle, the survivors of that session by the fire, rejoiced that he would be thrust into the heart of Paris in a piping time of peace, peace, said the uncle a veteran of four years of solid war, peace. God bless it.

 He set up in a small apartment overlooking the Champ de Mars and on the first day of autumn when the returning population was in full frenzy, in a copper-colored bar where he stopped early in the morning to drink chocolate and eat pieces of buttered bread which he paid for as he took them one by one off a round plate, as the streets were washed down and men in blue coats streamed in and out, he looked across the room to a bank of sunny windows where the white dusty light was coming in on Shannon and made her look like an Irishwoman in a Sargent portrait.

 Because she was so beautiful in her enlightened posture and expression, and because an intelligence radiated from her, he became very daring and approached the table, cup of chocolate in hand, a beautiful leather briefcase under one arm. He said, *"Sprechen Sie Deutsch?"* at which she smiled and then laughed, because if they had been two Texas longhorns standing there in the corner of the café it could not have been more obvious that both were Americans; the fact was like water pouring over a dam. They went out and walked away hours. His daring began to extend itself to a year's tenure. He fell in love with her, having the peculiar feeling which new kisses can bring, an overwhelming sense of being alive in the face of the present. The world became an energetic frame. It was almost like being the leading man in an opera. Within a week she had moved two wicker trunks into his apartment. She did ballet exercises in the middle of the floor while they talked. She could not have told him that the first night when they walked up the Champs Élysées and basked in the lights and September fountains, a red-bearded Rumanian architect sat staring at her former bed and cursed himself in Hungarian, French, and English, and eventually threw a glass of Scotch flat up against the wall.

And then she disappeared each morning, and came back only after dark, having danced every day down to exhaustion. Harry was writing music, at which he was becoming masterful, in which he was beginning to be able to do anything he wanted. By terrifying bouts of sustained work he was forcing the creation of a great bed of experience, so that in the strong frame and healthy body of his twenties could be found an old man who had lived since the turn of the century, and whose wisdom at the craft astounded and amazed even competitors and the nearly deaf. He could write pieces as deep and blue as a fjord, echoing and quiet, and he could write as red as he pleased. American jazz born of a rich heartland and the death of the wilderness. And strangely, the better he got, the better he got, with no chance of slipping. This stood even Shannon in awe. Once he had said, I can do anything, absolutely anything. I am almost a master, and she had looked mean and tough and said, You can do *nothing*, leaving the room in a fit of envy which meant he could have her for at least another six months until their powers evened out again and she was able to glide and swirl naturally and gracefully beyond the ecstatic points to which his labor had taken him. But he was going farther, and they both knew it.

Winter passed. They had an enormous electricity bill, for the lights burned late at night, with Harry bearing down on his blinding white music pads and then touching the piano as if he were stroking a horse. Shannon danced and danced, slept from exhaustion, and danced again, becoming like Harry one of the ones who did not return in quiet and sadness to the starting point with a series of exquisite memories and some first editions. She danced at the National Theater. His pieces were really performed. Sometimes he conducted, in a light gray and blue tweed suit and his tortoise-shell glasses, and when he turned at the close and faced an approving audience, their feet stamping, the timbers of the hall shaking as if the earth had quaked, it threw him off balance for weeks during which he stuffed himself with good food and could write only music which was so squeaky it sounded like rusty wheels in the high Gare du Nord, music which if played for the pigeons would have made them rise in intolerance and bend in a sheet of white and gray across the plane of Paris sky.

And he ran in the afternoon amid the blue which met buildings softly under the clouds, panting, pushing his glasses back on his face as they tried to fall to the ground. Eventually he built a routine of going all the way out to Neuilly and back, and as he got stronger it wrote Shannon in for another few months, for she could love only strength and could not face weakness. But it was so hard, to run and write, to eat like a beast and then starve, to make love until the dawn and then be fit only for the morgue, to be moved so by the music that it was like an electrocution, complete surrender and exhaustion.

That summer they went to Greece. The winter's rain seemed as far away as medieval European cities, and yet it was in one of these cities that Harry wrote in thundering clear classical style. He took the opportunity to take down good Greek music, and to write barrelhouse rolls to limericks they made up. These became extremely popular at a restaurant in New Epidavros called "Yellow House of Nonsensical Pleasure" where the foreigners gathered in the evenings. Of several dozen Swedes, Englishmen, French, Greeks, Americans, and Italians, three had birthdays on the same day, two (including Harry) had perfect pitch, all knew the fountain at Aix-en-Provence (or said they did), and everyone except the women except one was in love with Shannon—as if drawn into the maelstrom; the bright challenge took them up in its hands like moths.

Harry and Shannon slept on the roof; a phonograph played them to sleep. As they watched the stars they became separate. Harry knew she was in love with the doctor, an Oklahoman who had been broken in Vietnam and then come back stronger. He was both larger and wiser than Harry, although he could not compose music, and he called Harry "Spence." Next to him Harry felt like a young midget, and because he was not fresh or new at Shannon's game he lost early on in the subtle war of deferences at the Yellow House of Nonsensical Pleasure. Harry retired to the piano and played his barrelhouse rolls, and then stopped going there altogether, and then Shannon did not come up to the roof.

He cursed himself for not having the wisdom war brings. His father had told him of lying awake in an open meadow with an automatic rifle across his lap, waiting for the enemy while the sky was filled with artillery flashes and the white lightning of battle, a terror which numbed the little patrol in the field, something Harry might never know. It was one of the major reasons Harry loved his father, his sense early on that the man knew terror and bloodshed, and was grateful and loving just to be alive. They, the men in his family who had started out as merchants and professors and been made into warriors, knew something he could not. But they envied him for his cradle of peace. There was no way to compete with the Oklahoman, with the bronzed face and tranquil eyes which had seen men die in war. Harry was at a loss but determined to push with the same energy which had led them to survive, toward a depth in peace *they* could never know. He too was a fighter of sorts. To take in the whole great compass of the world—this was his task. The expanse of it could kill, and he had to dodge as best he could the potent backlash of music's ecstasy. He left for Paris precipitously, almost without thinking or looking back, and when he arrived he forwarded Shannon her wicker trunks, wondering what she would do with twenty-five pairs of dancing shoes in a wild rocky spine of the Peloponnesus. She had written that if she returned she would meet him at the Jeu de Paume at five o'clock on October 27, the day after her ticket expired.

It was already five-thirty. He could smell roasting chestnuts. He was in his light gray and blue suit, and he carried the leather briefcase under his arm. It was filled with musical manuscripts he had written since his return from Greece. He was steady, slept soundly, spoke softly, and smiled more. He was older, and he felt like his father, enjoying little things. His desk looked more chestnut-colored, and the bright lights of autumn were sharper than they had ever been. He knew now who was good, and he knew he was good. Massive clouds made the dark come early. Cold lightnings could be seen far north of Paris. High in the air birds rode thermals, tiny white flecks against the gray clouds. He loved the cool air, and looked up and down the paths, but they were emptying and the leaves just rustled on the floor of the Tuileries as if they were a German forest. That night he would sit under his lamp and pen the blinding white sheets; every day he felt himself rising a little higher, quietly, powerfully. He jumped off the railing and walked toward the Champs Élysées. He was due at dinner with a friend whose sister was to be there. He was in the Ministry of Finance and she was a model who had appeared on the covers of *Match, Jours de France* and *Elle*. One evening Harry had been in a restaurant alone and had stared at her picture, feeling himself fall into a trance somehow allied to the sweet darkness outside. My God, he said, as his heart opened to her image. The serenity was numbing. He found himself walking with quick step as a winter wind came down the Champs Élysées.

He passed a tall girl with a beret. That bittersweet frame and the cold rushing air, the leaves like percussion, made him shudder. His friend's sister had deep blue eyes and on the cover of *Elle* she had been wearing a blue velvet gown. He knew he would be loving her soon, in the quiet of autumn smooth, silent, and blue.

The River

James Laughlin

You can go on moving around, thinking it's the place and not you, for a good while, trying the mountains and this city and that, even trying English country, which is about as far as an American can go, and then finally after you've spent most of your money and worn out two or three typewriter ribbons without getting anything done, you begin to see and know that it's not the places it's just you. Then if you have any sense you go back to Springfield and teach school or try to get a job in the bank and pretty soon the outlying cousins are saying how that crazy Carson is settling down and maybe'll come to something after all.

Craig and I wouldn't have come to be saying we didn't have sense, but when we got to Paris along about August, knowing then it wasn't the fault of the places where we'd been, we knew we ought to give up and go home, but we knew even more we'd rather do anything else. And so, as Craig said, rather than go home and start brawling with our families again, we would just sit still in Paris watching the sun shine and the Seine flow, hoping it wouldn't rain more than two days a week. We did and it didn't. In fact it was about the best weather we'd had anywhere, good and hot so you knew it was summer all right but none of those stinkers that you get in Wisconsin and hardly any rain.

The Seine was dirty, so dirty we didn't dare try swimming in it for fear of catching something, but it did flow in a quiet steady way that made me feel at home. (I've never liked New York because the river isn't in the middle of it where it ought to be. For me it has always been that a city that is a city is a city built on two sides of a river with each side about equal in importance. And Paris is like that. There are more of what the tourist maps call monuments on the right bank, but on the left bank you see twice as many people who look good for something, which keeps the two sides balanced. Then there is Notre Dame in the middle being a fulcrum, that is, at least, as far as I'm concerned it's a fulcrum.)

In Salzburg, where we had been in July, we had gotten used to a rushing roaring river, a river fairly blowing its head off to get wherever it's going. Wherever we went in Salzburg, even when we were stymied by one of those little bergs that crop up like pimples all around the town, we could feel the Salzach plunging along, almost jumping out of its bed. It was an excited river, and we were excited too, excited by being face to face with our futures, really alone with our future lives for the first time. The Salzach was an excited river. One day as we were crossing it Craig described the Salzach perfectly: he looked down from the bridge at it and said, "Yessir, she'll be comin' round the mountain when she comes!"

So the Seine seemed quiet to us when we first got to Paris, quiet and a little contemptible. (You'll wonder why we even noticed the river in a big busy city like Paris, but I'll tell you that water is such a thing to me that wherever I am it is the thing I see first last and longest.) But soon we were liking it better, soon liking it very well as we walked slowly along the quais in the late evening as the lights came on, and soon we were knowing that its slow steady flowing pleased us perfectly. Our time came to be the Seine's time, and again and again I stopped when crossing a bridge to lean over the wall and watch for a long time the brown water moving and yet staying, speaking but silent, hurrying yet delaying.

In Salzburg our living had been like the river there, intense and driven. We thought then we were going somewhere and wanted to hurry. We were pushed and pulled, pushed by the memory of what life had been like at home, and pulled by the desire for success which would give us permanent escape. There was really nothing exceptional about our life at home (we lived in Springfield, Wisconsin); we were more or less typical—sensitive boys wanting to live a life of books and feeling smothered by the indifference of the people around us to the things we idolized. Springfield had a

The River

library, one of those Carnegie libraries that you find in small cities, but it had no books in it by Proust or James Joyce or Ezra Pound. Springfield had occasional concerts, but the pianists never played anything but Chopin and the singers sang "On the Road to Mandalay." There was an art shop in Springfield—it sold reproductions of "The Last Indian." There were pretty girls in Springfield but most of them thought Craig and I were flits and made us miserable; not one of them could have stood still or kept quiet for three minutes. How did we know about things like that? A teacher in the high school, a young English teacher. He was different. He came from the East. He understood. And Craig and I had become his intimates, draining from him his store of good things from the other world for which we came to long. We were with him constantly. He was a poet. And we were poets. We dreamed together—he was only seven years older than Craig and I—of life in Paris, of life in the hill towns, of a better, richer life far, far away from Springfield. Yet there was nothing exceptional in this; there are boys dreaming such dreams in every city in America. The exceptional thing was that we were able to try to live them, able to get away from the home we so despised while we were still young enough really to despise it.

It came about through Craig's grandmother. She persuaded our families to let us go. She understood us. She could not understand the books we read or the things we talked about but she could understand what was happening inside us and put some sort of true value on it. Our parents could understand it in a way—we were not the first boys in Springfield to get ideas. But to them our leanings were just a phase, something annoying, like the measles, through which we safely would pass in time, to be in the end like them. Oh they understood us well enough! They were decent as could be. They let us have money for books and did not mind our being continually with Charles Herrick, but they were never for us. They never really thought it would be a wonderful thing if one of us should turn out to be a famous writer, or that it would be a better thing than our turning out to be moneymaking businessmen. But Craig's grandmother did understand us. She had never known a poet in her life but she could think of our being such a thing without feeling self-conscious about it. She was a larger mind than the rest, not a more developed mind, but one larger to begin with, capable of a wider natural knowledge. She was not dissatisfied with life in Springfield but she could realize that there were other places in the world where life could be as good and even better perhaps. That our parents could not do. Their imagination did not go beyond having the best house in Springfield. They might have filled it with expensive paintings from Italy if they had made that much money—they were not hicks, they made trips to New York and to California—they simply never thought of life anywhere else being possibly life for them. I imagine that they would really have rejected France because it had few bathtubs.

But Craig's grandmother got around them. She liked us. Without herself being in any way a rebel she could appreciate rebellion. She could sense that a distaste for life in Springfield might not be a weakness in our characters. She liked us. We often brought Herrick to her house and overwhelmed her with our immensities of superior wisdom. It was all Greek to her—she was not bookish—but she liked it. And she persuaded our families to let us go when we'd been graduated from high school. She persuaded them by saying it would be the quickest way to get us over it, to let us go and rub our noses in it. "They'll come back after a year and go to college and that will be the end of it," she told our parents. But those were not her real feelings, that was just her craft, a craft in which she was being perfectly honorable because she felt it was for our good. She didn't think we would get over it. She hoped we wouldn't. She wanted more for us than success in Springfield.

I think though that what probably finally decided Craig's father and mine (they were close friends) to let us go was the idea of showing Springfield that they were well enough off to give us trips abroad before we began college. I think the phrase "grand tour" and something of its connotation had permeated into Springfield.

And so we went. We were in the odd class that finished high school in February and we crossed over in March. And July found us in Salzburg, full of excitement, and confident of the wonders ahead of us. We weren't ridiculous. We had a sense of humor, if it was a little undeveloped. We didn't think that one glimpse of an oxcart would turn us into geniuses, but we were sure that things

The River

would be different in Europe, that the barriers inside us that had kept us from writing anything more startling at home than fairly adept imitations would somehow be moved away by the new life. In America we had known that what held us back was the atmosphere and not something in ourselves.

And we still thought so in Salzburg, in spite of the barren weeks in Munich (nice old atmosphere and lots of culture but not too much diversion), the Dolomites (what we need are the primitive realities—rocks and peasants), Ragusa (get out of this damn rain, get the sun, life force), Vienna (blend of Teutonic and Celtic spirits, just the thing), and Budapest (need more color). We still didn't realize that the only thing that stimulated us was finding good excuses to disturb the travail of composition. Craig had gotten around to justifying his obscurity (somehow his lines didn't seem to have much "style" when they had also to make sense) by saying that psychoanalysis had driven poetry to associational logic, and I had actually reached Chapter XI in my autobiographical novel, although somehow my scene had managed to get itself shifted from Springfield to the more exotic quarters of Vienna. As I say, in Salzburg, with the Salzach running itself ragged beside us and inside us, we were still energetically stubbing our toes on our own heels.

And then we had seventeen hours in a smelly third-class carriage to Paris with plenty of time to think and no mask of atmosphere or ritual between ourselves and the mirror. We didn't talk about it at all, we didn't even discuss what we'd do in Paris, but when we got there we both knew, though we didn't admit it at first, that it wasn't the fault of the places we'd been but just ourselves. All day we sat watching the rain-soaked country go by, watching the rain fall steadily against the gloomy station walls where the train stopped, while more and more the forced confidence of our early-morning start faded into uncertainty and doubt melted into despair. And after night came, hiding the rain and locking us tightly into our stale-smelling wooden box, there wasn't the least struggle left in us, in either of us; we were done for and we knew it and we didn't care enough anymore to mind.

So soon the Seine seemed fine to us, as we were going no faster than it was, hardly moving at all, just letting ourselves be washed pleasantly along. At first we stayed at a fairly good hotel on the Quai Voltaire (the one where they say that an American lady saw a gendarme under her bed and moved right on to Berlin without saying a word) but that was too expensive and we moved to the Pretty Hotel in the Rue Amalie back near the Champ de Mars. It was an awful quarter to live in, not tough or dirty but just messy and sloppy, but the room was big and cheap and after all, as Craig said, if you couldn't afford the St James et d'Albany the next most distinguished certainly was the Pretty. We were there almost a week before we caught on to the nature of the Pretty's principal business, though two or three nights the banging around on the stairs had woken us up, and not having our own bathroom we thought we would be better off the quicker we ditched the Pretty, which we did.

Walking down the Rue Saint-Dominique one day we'd seen a Chambres-à-Louer sign hanging out a window and we went there. It was an insurance agent who had his office on the second floor of an old apartment house; he had the whole floor and there were some little rooms in the back that he didn't use. We got two for less than we had been paying for one at the Pretty, which suited me fine because, much as I like Craig I'd gotten tired of looking at his dirty shirts lying around in corners, and besides I have always hated to be looked at by anyone while I'm busy waking up in the morning. We almost moved again after a few days when we found out that one of the rooms down the hall belonged to a great big black man, but we finally decided that, as Craig said, miscegenation was better than moving again. So we stayed, and then in a few weeks we were calling the black man Josh and buying him drinks at the corner bistro while he told us about the war and all the French women he'd had in a mixture of broken-down French and even worse English that he'd picked up from an English spinster in Aries who had paid him well, he said, for just coming to sit with her of an evening. After getting out of the army, Josh had managed to marry a solid widow who politely had died at once leaving him enough to enjoy Paris for a few years before going home to his brother Senegalese.

So we stayed and the quiet waiting ways of Paris grew into us. We found a little restaurant in the quarter where they would cook eggs for us at ten in the morning, we got used to coffee with chicory in it, we learned the bus routes and got caught riding first class in the Métro, we didn't bother anymore to get our pants pressed, we began picking up some argot, and we even got used to keeping the covers on our typewriters all day.

As I say, the weather in Paris that August was all you could have asked for, sun every day but never so hot that you sweated when you walked the way you do in August back at home. We walked a lot, usually in the evenings when the coming darkness seemed to stir a breeze, not going anywhere in particular, just strolling along the quiet streets and busy boulevards, talking a little now and then about the things we saw, the people we passed and the houses, the people walking quickly to get somewhere, the people walking slowly as were we, the people sitting on little chairs before their doors, talking and watching, the houses we passed, the houses some hard, some soft, sometimes like pictures but more often not, walking and sometimes talking, walking slowly, talking lightly, not hurrying and not delaying, hardly thinking what we were saying; so walking and so lightly quietly talking, we often saw and surely came to know the way the light dies and the night comes softly on. And we sat.

We learned to like to sit and watch, to sit and sip, to sit and sit. For Paris is a sitting city.

There is no city anywhere that sits as Paris sits, that sits so much, so often, or so everywhere. And soon we were sitting and waiting, or sitting and worrying, as is the American way, but watching and gently talking. At first we sat when we were tired of walking and then we came to sit for sitting's sake. We sat a lot, in many places both by day and night.

We sat at big cafés on boulevards and at little ones on side streets. We sat on park benches sometimes and never on park chairs because we couldn't bear to pay the chairkeepers. In the mornings before lunch we would sit at one of the cafés near the Opéra, reading the paper and our mail if we had any, our mail from home that we rushed each day to the American Express office to collect and then never liked when we read it. We never liked them, the half angry half loving letters from our families back in Springfield, but we would always read them, each reading his own first and then reading it to the other. They didn't bore us or make us homesick, they only made us vaguely uneasy, because we knew that the life they told about would always be more real to us than that we were living, much as we hated it and wanted to escape from it. And they made us think of our families as we didn't want to, made us neither hate them nor love them, but only realize how wholly we were bound to them, how surely we would never cease to be what they had made us. We read our letters and then as we sat watching people come and go, sipping a vermouth or perhaps a Pernod, making up in our minds elaborate answers to them which we finally never wrote.

And as we sat and watched we read the *Paris Herald* through, first skipping from page to page, then reading every word. It was a daily ritual, completely meaningless and very satisfying, to read it all, to read the whole dull paper which was exactly the same every day. We read all the *Paris Herald* every day and never anything else, easily forgetting all about the solid classics in pocket editions that we'd carted around Europe to feed our souls on. We read everything in that paper and liked it. Just watching the news of the world floating by on the front page seemed to give us a sense of action, to establish us against time, and never did the editor fill space by printing the whole passenger list of an incoming liner but we read every name, never recognizing that of anyone we knew, but somehow enjoying the certain knowledge that these were their names. We read all the personal items in the society column and tried to figure out which ones had been sent in by the people themselves. Naturally, we had no way of telling, but sometimes from the name we could be sure it was that of a person who liked to see himself in print. We read the stupid Republican editorials that someone told us were written by Englishmen. We read the financial articles which we didn't understand. We read the letters from pacifists, puzzlemakers, amateur politicians, and ladies exchanging recipes, and thought up sarcastic answers to them which we never sent in to the paper. We read, as I say, the whole paper and liked it, but most of all two things: Sparrow Robertson and the baseball games. Back at home we would never have read the sports page at all as a matter of principle, but there in Paris at the big cafés, sitting and sipping, watching and reading, we came to be liking that part best of all.

There is one good reason why the *Paris Chicago Tribune* could never really rival the *Paris New York Herald* and that is Sparrow Robertson. You have got to read him to believe him possible. I suppose Sparrow Robertson would call himself a philosopher of sport, but to me he will just always be the great living master of American prose. If I were to quote things he has written, you wouldn't see what I was talking about. No, you have got to come on Sparrow Robertson's literary pearls by yourself, to stumble on them yourself in the middle of his dignified account of the last boxing match at the Palais des Sports or a hailstorm of statistics about horseracing results in 1910. Now I wouldn't want to give a wrong impression and have you think that Sparrow Robertson ever gave way to unnecessary rhetoric or even sporting jargon, because he is, I assure you, a very serious artist indeed. No, it is only that sometimes his enthusiasm for expression, his great affection for his subject leads Sparrow by the way of certain lapses of grammar, certain variants from the accepted order, which are so individual, or let us say, so quite apart, in fact so gorgeously and beautifully things unto themselves that there is I assure you nothing in the heavens nor on earth to measure the joy, the orgasmic abdominal joy, with which the reader thereof is instantaneously seized. For you see old pal Sparrow has a way of saying things that is really kinda funny.

But it was really the baseball that mattered most. As I remember that time it is this that I remember, the passionate way we felt about the Cardinals slowly catching up on the Giants. Now I couldn't even tell you who finally did win the pennant that year, in fact I think in the end it wasn't either the Cardinals or the Giants, but still there is something left in me of the way I was feeling about it then, the passionate death-and-destiny way I was feeling about the Cardinals slowly catching up with the Giants. There was no obvious reason for liking one team better than the other, but somehow the verbiage of the sportswriters who were playing up the race between them did its work on us, and we began to feel excited and concerned. Neither of us had ever been in St. Louis, but really the teams didn't mean places to us anyway. They didn't mean places or even ideas to us, it was their slow steady struggle, the tortured rising and falling of their percentages as they won and lost games, the gradual catching up, the sudden spurts ahead and falling back, the agony or joy of two games won or lost on the same day, the nervousness of games divided, the exciting certainty that the Cardinals would finally catch up mixed with the worrying doubt that their luck might change and they wouldn't, these were the things that were meaning so much to us then, this constant excitement of fighting against chance, assurance against doubt, ourselves and the Cardinals against the Giants and luck. It seems foolish that we should have cared at all, and yet even now, when suddenly something makes that time come back inside me, I can feel a little of the feeling that we had, the tense exciting feeling that we had.

So our morning sitting wasn't quiet, when we read the papers and the letters from home. But in the afternoons we had a very different kind of quiet pleasant sitting.

Then we went into little hidden streets, where at deserted bistros bad-tempered old women would serve us dirty glasses of stale beer that we could hardly swallow. In gray and dusty side streets we sat away our afternoons; watching the people come and go who don't walk for pleasure, watching the flow of life that does not see itself because its living is too close and real. Mornings and evenings we saw Gay Paree, but afternoons we saw Chelsea and the East Side, every shabby street from South Boston to Bucharest, empty of life and full of living, the quickslow fatlean oldyoung shabby ones who have no names. We sat and saw them endlessly ever and never the same, an endless broken-rhythmed movement from somewhere to somewhere and nowhere to nowhere. Each time we saw the kind of face or step or look we thought we knew, we knew the more we knew nothing. We thought we knew where we were, and then we weren't so sure; we only knew this moving, this coming and going, slow steady flowing from nothing to nothing, from zero to infinity. Dusty sunlight in a faded street.

"What does it mean, Craig, where are they going, where are we going?"

"You tell me, why don't you!"

Dusty sunlight and the noises far and near, city sounds that rise and fall and never die, a voice of many tones, speaking the words we hear but cannot understand.

"What can we do, Craig, to make it stop for a minute to make the whole damn thing stop and look at us for a minute?"

"You're asking me?"

Dusty sunlight and the feeling of old stone and the feeling of blood, not the quick blood of a wound, but the slow, stale blood of life's endless seepage. "Look, Craig, look at that dog over there in the gutter; it's free! It doesn't see what we see! It doesn't have to try to understand!"

At night we sat at the big cafes in Montparnasse and tried not to look like Americans. "We can never do it," Craig used to say, "until we get suits with pointed lapels and stop wearing crépe-soled shoes." We would have liked to do the boîtes on Montmartre, but we didn't have the money to waste; we had to go places where we could sit for a long time without spending much. So we sat at the Dôme and the Rotonde and wondered what they had been like in the good old days before all the Americans went home to Connecticut. There were still young Americans to be seen around in various states of intoxication, but they none of them looked as though they might be Hemingways or Harry Crosbys or McAlmons. Most of them looked as though they might be medical students or bank clerks, and certainly none appeared to be wearing the black hat very hard. We sat at the bright noisy corner and tried not to look like Americans, while we talked about nothing else except America, and why we were Americans and what it meant and what we were going to do about it. I don't remember what we said anymore; there was a lot of talk about time concepts and the sensuality of motion, about the abstractions of materialism and deracination, about lack of resistance by tradition and even the melting pot. There was endless talk about the American Scene and Pure Art, and of it all I remember almost nothing. It was serious and completely unimportant, and we forgot what we had said one night in time to say it again the next. We sat and watched and knew that we were waiting for something to happen, as every American must wait for something to happen, and gradually grew more and more content to have what was to happen be nothing happening at all. Almost we ceased to care to think we knew what we were waiting for. We sat and watched.

Naturally, as you might expect, the great diversion of our evening sitting was that of watching the girls. Back home in Springfield we had always heard the usual stories about the women of Paris, and now that we were there seeing them, we could see that there was a reason for all the talk. As Craig said, having looked over the Françaises he could understand why the frogs didn't want the Germans to get Paris. Sitting there at the Dôme and the Rotonde we saw some mighty interesting specimens, and seeing them we were wishing all the time that we were a lot richer and more experienced and less generally terrified of something that had been a continual source of speculation for years without ever ceasing to be a hopelessly insoluble problem. And so we watched and joked, savoring in imagination the thing we wanted but didn't dare to touch. It wasn't that both of us hadn't had the usual adolescent experiences, or that we didn't know, or think we knew, about all there was to the subject, but somehow there was an impassable barrier between the Springfield high school girls whom you pawed in rumble seats and the Paris ponte who stared at you with unconcealed contempt. And so we sat and watched and wondered, yearning with mind and body, trying vainly to believe that we were being sensible and mature and only succeeding in feeling more intensely the frustration of our immaturity.

It's true that we did have one mild adventure but that only served to increase our discontent, increasing desire without increasing confidence or removing doubt. It was nothing extraordinary—two obviously nonprofessional young females who gave us the eye one night as we were walking across the Champ de Mars and picked us up when they found we didn't have the *savoir-faire* to do it ourselves. At this point Craig took control of the situation, attaching to himself the better looking of the two and leading the way down one of the more obscure and less public paths of the gardens that lie beneath the Eiffel Tower. I can't say that I had a particularly good time. The girl was too eager and I was clumsy with her, but at least I found that the difference in language was a great help. Trying to say something in situations where absolutely nothing was to be said had always given me an unnatural horror of them. But that night, having only to talk with lips and hands, above all knowing that I would never have to see the girl again, I had less separation of mind and body, less the feeling of being a ridiculous fool. But after my heat had risen and then cooled, when repeated caresses were no longer a crescendo that swept along the mind, in the body's ascent, when kiss after kiss was like the banging of a bad chord, mere product of inertia, when nothing remained of the first excitement but a boredom half disgust; when I had suddenly left the girl without a word, pushed her away, risen, turned and gone away in a single motion, walking as fast as I could without once looking back until I had come to the edge of a river; then, as I slowly went along the bank, watching the water moving in the spots of mirrored light, feeling the stillness of the silent river in the sleeping night, I felt again, as I had felt before, that these things I had done, the things that had been done to me, could never really have importance, could never be all to me that I wanted them to be, all that I had read and sensed that they could be, until the person for whom they were done and who did them was one speaking to more of me than the body alone. For all of its being in Paris this was no more to me than had been similar experiences in the country roads outside of Springfield. It increased my desires without giving me any greater reason for them.

But with Craig it was otherwise, for he told me next day, though I had done everything I could to keep him from bringing up the subject, that his girl had been a "pretty hot little number" and that she had "given him a real good workout considering it was free." And I could see that the thing had started up in him a new kind of inside movement that had not been there before, for from then on, though he didn't say it, I could see that the half unhappy pleasure of our quiet watching waiting life in summer Paris was no longer so much for him as it had been. He began to get restless and he didn't talk in the same way as he had been talking; I could see that there was a separation taking place inside him and that he was no longer content to be drifting without a good American goal to hold on to. I could see growing in him the need to be working toward something definite. I could feel the American in him coming back to rule him, could see him beginning to feel that time was wasted in which something wasn't done and that walking and talking, sitting and sipping, watching and waiting, were not enough to make a completed life. He didn't start to work again at his poetry, but he read again and seemed hardly to notice the quiet life around him but only to notice the busy moving life, to realize that time was going on without him. He was changing, as I say, and I could see it but I didn't say anything, because I knew that it would only make it go faster. I knew what the change would be, and was sorry for it.

Somehow I knew the day on which he would go, the boat on which he would sail, before he even tried to break the news to me. And somehow he sensed from the way I answered him, that there was no need for him to explain anything, that I quite understood and that I would not try to change his mind. I didn't and he bought his ticket. We agreed that he would tell my parents that I had joined up with two English boys whom we had gotten to know in Paris who were "very steady and quite all right," so that they wouldn't think I was alone and try to make me come home, and that he would spread the word around Springfield that I was putting the finishing touches on a novel that a big London publisher was waiting to publish. Craig left me his American razor blades, and the night before he sailed we celebrated the end of our partnership with champagne, but as we could only afford a half-bottle, we neither of us managed to work up much gaiety. I was sorry to see him go, but not as much as I should have expected if I'd known it was going to happen two months before. We have always been each other's best friend, and we still are, but somehow it seemed to me perfectly natural that we should come apart just as we had gone together, casually almost without any sentiment or excitement. Craig said he would write, and I knew he wouldn't and knew as well that the moment I saw him again we would be right away as good friends as ever we had been. So Craig went home the third week in September, and I stayed on in Paris with the slow-flowing Seine and the shadow of black Josh down the hall.

As the boat train was pulling out of the Gare St. Lazare, Craig leaned out the window and started to spout some sort of slush about what our being together had meant to him, but I said, "Stuff it,

Alexander, stuff it!" and Craig laughed and shouted, "O.K., Boss," as the train rolled away from me down the platform.

For about a week after Craig had gone I felt as though something inside me was going around without any clothes on, but soon it began to get itself dressed, and by October Craig had gotten to be for me just part of Springfield, though often at unexpected moments I suddenly remembered things about him—the way he had of summing up a discussion with a bad epigram and the way he had of running his fingers along a wall or a fence when we were walking.

I had a long letter from him from the boat full of unconvincing explanations which seemed entirely natural. He said that of course it had been a wonderful experience, and that he couldn't thank me enough for all the help I had been to him, but that he was convinced that, although he would always want to live a life of the spirit and the intellect, he wasn't really gifted for poetry and that probably he had just mistaken sensitivity for something more. He ended up by saying that he knew I had real talent and that I shouldn't let myself be discouraged by what he imagined was just a normal interval of lying fallow.

I didn't reread his letter, but I didn't throw it away, because I could see that he'd spent a lot of time on it, probably making two or three drafts to get it right.

Then there was the letter from Springfield saying that the town hadn't razzed him half as much as he'd expected and that most of the people were really a good deal better sort than he'd thought. Later he wrote from Chicago that his father had agreed to put him through the university so that he could get a teaching job, and then there was nothing for about five months, until I got one of those fancy engagement announcements in two envelopes. It was a girl I'd never liked much, but her father had a big drygoods business and she'd been East to school. On the corner of the card Craig had written in pencil "How'm I doin?" with three big dollar signs after it. I thought about the dollar signs and thought about some of the poems he had written, and then I didn't think anymore because I saw there was really nothing to think about.

For a while after Craig had gone I went on with my quiet life, watching the flow of the city living, slow as the flow of the river, waiting for nothing, as the Parisians seemed to be waiting for nothing, and as their river the Seine seemed not to be knowing that it was flowing or where it was going. For a while, I say, things were as they had been, except that I was doing them alone and a little sadly. And then I too began to change, though not as Craig had changed. I didn't rebel at the movement around me, or fight against it as he had done, I simply began to become a part of it, to move with it and in it, to go as it flowed, to be one with it. Still I was watching the waiting, but now the two were one thing; the watching became my waiting. I was no longer waiting for nothing because I was watching, but because my watching was in time with my waiting, I was not waiting as Americans wait, waiting for something to happen, I was waiting as Parisians wait, awaiting nothing and yet always having something, having my watching and then finally another thing— my telling.

Yes, again the top came off my typewriter and I bought hundreds of sheets of white paper, and again my writing began. But now it was different than it had been before, it was a part of the very flowing it described. It was no longer a means to something, but something itself, no longer something I was waiting to have happen, to have succeed, to win me fame and escape from Springfield; it was, as I say, no longer this to me, it was a constant part of life to me, something I did each day as I ate and sat and talked and watched and waited. It came to be not telling life for me, but part of life itself for me.

And so as fall came on and the heat of summer fell away, I came to be working every day, telling the things I saw and what I thought I knew about them, making a picture of this slow and steady movement, this gradual onward flowing, this simple waiting that I felt and lived. As the leaves fell and the nights grew cold, as each day the lights came on a little earlier, as each day the air told more of winter's coming, as each day there was less struggle inside me between what remained of the life at home and what was building of my own life. I came to have, to really have and really know, what we had tried so hard to find and never found, I came to be a writer and began to be a man.

The Highly Prized Pajamas

Robert McAlmon

Girls such as Yoland used to be called of the half-world, though it can not be explained why their world is more half than the world of aristocrats, workers, or the bourgeois, few of whom take so much into the range of their experience as Yoland did.

She was about the Latin and Montparnasse quarters for two years before people commented upon her archaic Greek beauty. I associated her with a type of low-class *poule*, who without mind and abandoned, soon grows bloated and ugly and disappears. One may hear of them as dying of consumption back in little villages, on farms; or one may forget to remember if they are mentioned. Integral a part as they are of the French social organism, no one, or one year's crop of them, is essential. Each season brings its new recruits.

Yoland went about with Andra, of young pig-faced charms, and Arlette, who, darkly striking, soon disintegrated into bovine aspects and was soddenly drunk nightly until she became consumptive and disappeared. Any of the three was apt to be in some bar at any time of day, from noon till five in the morning. There was little outward evidence that they were plying their trade. However, they had money to drink on, dressed well, and rather than gold-dig off foreigners they were inclined to gather in flocks with others of their kind. Their laughter taunted like that of so many hyenas as they sat before their drinks, jeering and laughing at the strange habits of foreigners.

Seated in the Parnasse bar, which was empty but for Jimmie, the barman, I was having a sandwich and a beer when I noticed a copy of Proust's *Sodome et Gomorrhe* on the table next to mine. I picked it up to scan and Yoland came from the ladies' room to stand waiting for me to hand her the book. I was surprised that a girl of her sort should be reading that, so I asked her to have a drink. She would, and sat down. When I asked if she liked to read she crackled a dry, inhuman laugh, unlubricatedly metallic. Mechanically the laugh had cuteness.

"I don't like sentimental things. Sometimes I read. This," she indicated the book, "is of things we all know if we aren't stupid. The author I wouldn't like," her rusty crackle of laughter sounded, "but he wouldn't like me. He liked only men. His heroine is a man he has made a woman in the book, but I like his manner."

It occurred to me that I'd underrated Yoland's perceptions considerably. We chatted, but she had no intention of telling much about herself to a stranger. Thoughts of her past apparently irritated her. She did say that until she was thirty or no longer good-looking she would live a life of freedom, abandon, if people wanted to call it that. She didn't want marriage, or family life, and why should she give up freedom to become settled or a woman of the home? She knew when young more than she wanted to know of these things.

As we sat, a photographer who liked doing studies of unusual looking people came into the place. I asked him to sit with us, and said, as Yoland did not understand English, "Have you ever noticed how beautiful Yoland is? A more perfect and delicate profile doesn't exist, and her eyelashes are really long and black. It isn't maquillage."

Her teeth too were straight, not too small, and glistening white, and her eyes large, and softly grey if one didn't detect that their softness was no evidence of a tender nature. The photographer, as we sat analyzing her perfections, agreed, and asked her if she would pose for him.

"My body is not good," she said finally, assuming at once that he meant for her to pose in the nude. "I have more than enough breast, and my waist is not subtle."

When assured that he wanted to photograph her face, three quarters or profile, she agreed, and said she often made money posing for romance photographs one can buy in postcard shops. The idea amused her; she mimicked sweet young love poses she had taken for these pictures. Incidentally she appraised the photographer with her soft gaze, not assuming that he wished too to make love with her, but she informed me later, to judge whether she was willing if it came to that, and whether he was another man who pretended he wanted her as a model when he had other intentions. With such, she declared, she was ruthless.

The photographer left and Yoland's cute, unhuman laugh creaked after him. It struck her as droll that he should want to photograph her when she had posed for so many sentimental postcards which sell as a joke or to simple-minded people. "You know his friend, that dirty old man with white hair who would be droll if he was a Negro?" she asked, chortling, menacingly this time. "He asked me to pose for him, and they say he is famous. I believed he wanted a model. He showed me screens and pictures," she shrugged her shoulders. "I didn't care for them. He was to pay me two hundred francs for the afternoon. But the foolish old man thought he could make love to me too. I was cold and said 'no' and meant no, but he battled with me. Then I showed him my nails, on this hand." The nails on her hands were long and sharply pointed. "I can handle them when they get difficult. I would have torn the skin off his face, and then I said, 'You give me two thousand francs, and I will go. I tear your face, and call the police.' Never before have I done that. I don't like that sort of thing, but if he thought he could be brutal to me I would show him."

Yoland didn't need to inform me that she was hard. She wasn't apache class, but she had many of the tricks. I'd seen her break a glass and threaten to thrust its broken rim into the face of a man who annoyed her; and had heard her quarrelling with some girl she did not like. Then she had been aflame with cold menace.

Yoland evidently decided that she liked me, as a comrade, though she didn't like Americans generally. She wasn't flattered by my remarking on her beauty; she rather wondered why I commented on it now, when we had seen each other about for over a year. Just now she had the idea that she was making me think her cruel, and said, "I am *sensible* with those having emotions and sensibility, but usually I find little use for sentiment in this life."

"Independence of spirit is a quality I like too," I told her.

Her unlubricated rusty laugh chortled and she looked at me mockingly. "Ah, yes, you are independent, but as a passion."

Her remark struck home, and I hoped that one more clear realization of needless lack of detachment had functioned into my emotions.

After this she and I were comrades whenever we met and hadn't more intimate friends with us; we sat together and chatted pleasantly, without inquiring into each other intimately. Yoland drank copiously, and stayed up most nights till five o'clock. Her laughter mingled with that of other girls to make hyena noises. She threw glasses, cursed out the *patrons* and *patronnes* of bars and restaurants, and she was not unique in doing these things. However, she began to dress better, and people were soon commenting on her beauty. It was when she came forth in a pepper-red coat and dress, wearing a hat made of shiny black cock feathers that curled above her forehead and about her ears, that her profile stood out luminously white and perfect. Her teeth, when she smiled, were the perfection of dentifrice and glistening beauty; and her deep grey eyes glowed, but were aware people knew that their glow came from the dilation of drugs rather than from emotion stirring within her. In the emotion of anger they flashed hatred as she glared through her narrowed lids.

Yoland had, as had many others, fought with so many of the *gerantes* in the various cafés and bars in Montparnasse that she was a well-known figure to the police. When a small and stuffily cozy bar opened near the Jardin du Luxembourg she changed her rendezvous spot; so did many old-time Quarterites, to follow Jimmie the barman, who went to work there. Jimmie, a Liverpool Irishman, and an ex-prizefighter, was genial, tittered readily at the careless habits of his clients, was openhearted, and informed of the open-secret lives, amorous and financial, of about everyone in the Quarter. Eight years before this time he had arrived, naïf to Paris and full of alive curiosity. His first night he got drunk too, and seeing a fire-signalling box, banged it, and stood. Not then understanding French he didn't know what he had done. But the firemen arrived and wanted to know where the fire was. Jimmie didn't understand, but

The Highly Prized Pajamas

the police understood Jimmy, and he spent three weeks in the Prison de la Santé. When liquored up he was apt to remember his fighting days, and insist upon "protecting" friends he drank with. Sometimes his protection resulted in a night in jail for both Jimmie and his friend, but as the police took him with an ironic sense of comedy his sojourn with them was seldom overnight. When his blood pressure was too high from overeating and drinking, Jimmie had a habit of going to his room, banging his own nose so that it would bleed, and thereby reducing his blood pressure. Sometimes he would slit the lobes of his ears to lose more blood. In all, Jimmie suffered the pangs of loving and losing, and was a barman prone to understand the habits and attitudes of his clients in all their various types of drunk-ons.

In the New Bar Yoland collected an Argentinian lover. She wasn't attracted to him, but he persisted; he was wealthy; he gave her expensive clothes and jewelry; he gave her money, paid her apartment rent, and submitted to her tempers, so she accepted him for a time. He, José, was a thin, fidgety man, given to drinking vast quantities of pernod, but he seldom ate. When intoxicated he wanted to dance, and humped epileptically about the room, singing. The song was always the same. "Toreador, Toreador." His rendition was one apt to irritate anybody, let alone a nervous person. It surely irritated Yoland and one night José found himself sitting on the floor with a sore jaw. He'd sung one "Toreador" too many and Yoland slammed him. From then on she was apt to beat him up nightly, until it was a bar joke and comic even to Yoland. As fist-hits from her seemed only to please José, she took to scratching his face with her lengthy fingernails. The Madame of the bar would take him upstairs, put plasters on his face, and José came down ready for more punishment from his ladylove.

It became too much for Yoland, however. He bored her; he drove her wild; she crashed a broken glass into his face one night, tore from her neck an expensive pearl necklace he had given her, threw it at him, and departed. José was disconsolate, but as Yoland was not to be located for several weeks he moved elsewhere, and was out of her life. She, hearing of this, began again to make the bar her nightly rendezvous. She stayed in the hotel above. Madame Camille, thinking that Yoland would find José when she needed money badly, permitted her bill to mount, but when she argued that some amount of the bill should be paid, there was a violent quarrel. Madame Camille indiscreetly suggested that it was like stealing not to pay one's bill.

"You dirty cow," Yoland spit at her. "I am not a thief. That remark you will pay for," and a series of glasses flew in Madame Camille's direction. She hid behind the counter, too afraid to say she would call the police. Yoland, highly insulted, stopped her when she tried to make a placatory remark, for Madame Camille knew she'd never get money if she stayed enraged.

"Madame Camille," Yoland said frozen with hauteur, "I will not dispute further with you. You are a woman without education or breeding." At this she went out and took a taxi to haunts in another part of town. She was not seen about the Quarter for several months, and when she returned it appeared that she was amply provided for from the elegant clothes she sported. Seated at the Dome bar one afternoon Yoland chatted amiably, when Madame Camille appeared with a look of insecure triumph on her face. At last she had found Yoland and might collect what was owing her. Yoland was frigidly courteous, but Madame Camille got nowhere with her. She did finally get an address, however, and went away, saying that she would call on Yoland to collect.

Yoland's eyes were stony black with rage. "She calls me a thief. Ha, ha, la, ha," her menacing laugh rattled deathbones. "I did not give her my address. I gave her the address of my friend, and he will break her face in if she comes."

Yoland passed through a period of being *"une femme sérieuse"* while she lived with a wealthy Egyptian for several months, and she confided that at last she had found the race which knows how to make love. Before, love-making had been more or less of a bore to her. However, the Egyptian left, and she then lived with a forty-year-old Polish man, who, to my amazement, Yoland permitted to strike her in the face without her using either fingernails or broken glasses on him. Later she said that he was irrational. He was very gentle, but when he drank much he went crazy because of shell shock. "It is not me he hits at. It is a crazy something he sees," she said, and shrugged her shoulder, thinking me foolish to suppose she'd mind being beaten up under such circumstances. Could one fight back at a crazy man? He gave her a squirrel coat and various pieces of jewelry; and their romance was either successful or not, in that Yoland never got to the point of doing him physical damage. He, however, departed after some months, and Yoland was again about the Quarter daily. She now did only the better-class bars, and came into them generally alone. Andra, her pig-faced ex-friend, was about, and a very successful bourgeoise *poule*, but to none of her two-year-ago girl friends did Yoland pay any attention. She wasn't curt. She had decided that what amused them in life didn't amuse her, and she, instead of having lost her looks, was more elegantly and glisteningly beautiful than ever. Her pallor glowed; her teeth had a diamond sparkle, and she had learned what a hat and a color could do to give her beauty a setting. Nevertheless before long she was hard up. She'd grown more definite and positive in her tastes. I wondered if she was calming down and yearning for a settled and secure circumstance.

2

I found one day waiting for me a letter from Arthur Stout, who had been given my address by a friend. He had no reason to look me up except that he did not know Paris and I might tell him what to see and what to avoid. Also he understood that I was the friend of a psychoanalyst and interested in the subject myself, and as he had a deep affection (platonic, of course) for a woman who did not care for men he would like to talk to somebody more worldly than himself. A book-lover and scientist, he hadn't sampled any variety of life.

One gets used, in Paris, to having acquaintances and friends of friends think of residents as convenient guides and hosts, and I felt no inclination to conduct this unknown Mr. Stout to sights and other places I'd seen or didn't care to bother about. However, liking the man who'd given him my address, I dropped a note saying that he would be apt to locate me at the Coupole bar at aperitif hour almost any night. My morning letter reached him that day, for when

I went into the Coupole the barman told me that the gentleman in the corner had inquired for me.

Stout presented himself and offered me a drink. He was quiet-looking, and I understood at once that it is hard for a man not speaking French to get around in Paris at first, and Stout confessed that he had only one week before sailing back to America. "And I have three thousand dollars with me and don't care if I spend it all. There's more where it came from. I rather gathered from Morris (our friend) that you'd be the chap to locate an attractive sort of girl to keep me company when I'm at loose ends. In any case, whenever you or any of your friends are with me, all the bills for eating or drinking are mine."

I didn't jump off the barstool and run outside to blow the fire whistle, but certainly during the course of the evening I let various regulars of the always-broke quota know what had come upon us. It seemed cruel on Mr. Stout, but Morris should too have informed him that Montparnasse, where deadbeating is an art, is no place where he need make an offer such as the foregoing.

Mr. Stout said that he'd just come from the Riviera where he had read Frank Harris' *Life and Loves*. As I'd never more than glanced at the book, and then not to be interested, excited, or amused, we couldn't go far into that subject. Next Stout spoke of a cellar where Verlaine, Baudelaire, and others had once sat in discussion while drinking absinthe. He spoke of Dr. Hirschfield of Berlin, of sexual variants, and asked, reticently, what curious places there were to visit in Paris. Not too decisively I concluded that he was in search of subtle, aromatic vice, as imagined through literary gleanings. He obviously was a small town product, and showing me his notebook of addresses such as college boys, Legionnaires, and businessmen collect, he wanted me to tell him about the various places. As most of them were of *bourdelles* where people go to see poses, or for mass promiscuity—mainly for tourists—his interest lapsed, so I told him of more exotic places. He looked only mildly physical and sensuous, and his manner was slowly kind. It was probable, I thought, that he was merely sentimental and afraid that he was missing experience in life. Again he spoke of wanting a girl, and an aware, worldly girl, with intelligence.

Yoland came into the Coupole and spoke to me as she seated herself at the end of the bar. She smiled enigmatically. I concluded she had been taking heroin or opium, because though her smile seemed directed at me I knew she wasn't even looking at me. But her gleaming teeth glistened blue-white between her lips incarnadine, and as she turned to arrange her jet locks beneath her hat her clear profile gleamed white against the shiny shadow on the mirror.

"Who is that girl?" Stout asked, and there was tensity in his curiosity now, where before he had been merely casual.

I concluded that Yoland was a good answer for him.

At my suggestion Yoland came over to drink with us, and Stout admired the crystal clarity of her skin, and the modelled perfection of her facial contours. He couldn't speak much French, and I had to translate between then. Yoland noticed Stout's admiration and looked at me to chortle a low metallic crackle. I told her that he found her grey eyes lovely, faunlike, and tender, that he was sure she had a sweet and tender nature. She chortled cutely again, and her long eyelashes swept down over her drug-dilated eyes which had such liquid beauty. I suggested to Stout that he'd better not be too moved by Yoland, to listen to her laugh as much as he believed the mysterious glowing in her eyes. He was appearing altogether too much the small-town man in middling years wanting to break loose, and if Yoland had been taking drugs, she might get him into some row that he couldn't handle. I had no intention of spending the evening with them. Every warning I might give Stout, however, but further interested him in Yoland.

"I know by her face that she has an old soul," Stout said. "I don't go in for reincarnation, but I knew when you came into the bar that you had an old soul too. I knew it was you before you spoke though nobody had ever described you."

His talk would sometimes have made me uncomfortable, but I felt easy, knowing that soon the night aperitif crowds would be filling the place. I told Yoland that Stout wanted me to tell her that she was beautiful, and she merely rattled her machine laugh, knowing that she was so, and that I knew the matter didn't much interest her since so many people who liked her beauty irritated her.

"He likes you very much," I translated.

She asked, "He is rich?"

"Enough. He's ready to spend quite a sum of money while he's in Paris. He wants you to have dinner with him."

"Very well. I need a new coat, and dresses. I'm disgusted with the clothes that dirty pig José bought me. If he would see me in them he might still think he could come and speak to me." She observed Stout with a sidewise glance. He was charmed. "He is nice. He is sentimental, but that does no harm for a few days, since he goes in a week," she concluded.

Stout took her land to kiss, and wanted me to tell her that it was an aristocrat's hand, that he knew she had lived before. She leaned towards him and straightened his coat collar with a caressing pat, and looked at me again to chortle dry rattling laughter.

"I love her laugh," Stout said. "You say she is Basque? They are a race thousands of years old. She has lived many times before. Her laugh is cleared of emotions."

"Go careful on her temper though. See her fingernails. She keeps those on the right hand long and pointed to tear strips off a person's face when she's in a fight. Well-kept hands and nails are fairly general with French girls."

"Ask her why she has never married, if she intends to marry. Say she is too beautiful to live this kind of life."

"She might resent it. She is not given to thinking of herself as a lost soul. But I'll ask her about the marriage part."

"I want liberty," Yoland said curtly, and relaxed a little. "I don't love love if it binds me. What would there be for me to do if I was married?" She left us for a few minutes and when she returned the pupils of her eyes were huge black; she had put on more *maquillage* too, and looked smarter because her black hair was sleekly peeping from under the rim of black cock feathers on her hat. Quickly she saw that I noticed this, and crackled a laugh that came out in sharp hard spurts of metallic sound. Her glance agreed that it was funny that she should be acting coquettish because she saw that the simple, sentimental Stout expected that of her. She wondered at me too, that I asked her questions about her life, her family, and her first experience in love. Although she knew I was merely translating for Stout she didn't connect that type of question with me. She, however, answered, since she knew me well enough for two years past.

"He thinks that he will be serious with me," she jeered, cutely taunting. "When I was fourteen, I was seduced by a woman. Women didn't and don't interest me, but no matter. Soon after I seduced my seventeen-year-old boy cousin. And before either—" she hesitated before she decided to say the last, "I had known my father that was since I was twelve. In every case I was willing."

"And your mother?" I asked, having translated her remarks to Stout.

"My mother? I don't know. A country woman. She was not a wife. My father's family took me. He said I was mature and beautiful at twelve. At fifteen I was disgusted with my town and my father's home. He was old; he handled me. I didn't hate him, but I didn't want him, so I went away with an older woman and she wanted me to become a coiffeuse." Yoland laughed, harshly disdainful. "Me, a coiffeuse! I did not like small villages and I do not like people enough to fuss over old women's hair. Always I intended to come to Paris, to be free, and abandoned if I liked. You may tell him I am sufficiently well educated. My father has money and would send it to me but I want nothing more to do with that old man. I know life is nothing. Never have I expected anything of life. For me it is amusing only to be in bars and cabarets and with people who pretend no class."

"Let me read your hand?" I said, lightly curious.

"No, no," she answered, with a quick hardness, drawing her hand away. It was the first evidence of anything noncynical or superstitious I had detected in her. "Why should I be curious about my future? I take what comes and will always do so." Again she said that at thirty, or if she lost her looks or health, she might consider marriage, but that was eight years to wait yet.

"She is damned quick," Stout admired her. "The old race knowledge. She has lived before. It's my luck to fall for girls who like their own sex, I guess." His mild Teutonish face had a pleased expression. "She likes me, though. I don't know why." Yoland responded easily as he stroked her arms, and she smiled her glistening, mechanically glamorous smile, into his eyes, he thought, but she was looking at Andra too, with whom she had taken up anew in the last few days while she had been in financial difficulties. If she drank she might get rid of Stout and go away with Andra who had some attraction for her. Possibly the young pig-faced Andra took drugs with her.

Stout was evidently hoping that he was the man to awaken a soul in this girl, and as that is a hope aged with tradition I was glad that Yoland and Stout were holding hands and no longer asked me to translate back and forth. Other people came into the bar, among them four men I knew well, and with them I was wandering off to dine when Stout reminded me that I and all my friends were to be his guests if we wished. We waited, and had more drinks. Sporty, the hearty, hardy, and more generally used girl of the Quarter, came in, and she too joined us, and we all went to L'Avenue for dinner.

As Stout and Yoland kept gazing at each other Sporty engrossed the interest of the other five men. She told Groenlun that she would pose for him for nothing, but her face, he could see, was battered. She had been drunk three nights before and had fallen downstairs onto her face. But her body was not cut. No, no lover had beaten her this time. Later she confided to the party's youngest man that she knew a very rich man who liked boys, and who liked her too. "We will sleep three, non?" she asked the boy with generous hope.

The boy looked shy and indicated that he was not interested. "You no like?" Sporty accepted his rebuff with three of her ten words of English. "No go. Hello, goodbye then." She had as usual done her best to arrange things so that as many people as possible could enjoy themselves in this human world of ours, but with her sweet peasant sympathy for all desires, she understood not wanting everybody too. She decided to leave us, and as she was Sporty, with catholic tastes, she was sure to find company for the evening. With her departure we others left Yoland and Stout together, as Yoland wanted to go to La Cloche. By eleven o'clock they came back to La Coupole, however, and came up to me. Yoland was laughing her unlubricated laugh, steadily now as she was intoxicated. The jeer and taunt in her weird laugh wasn't at anybody in particular so much as it was at everybody, at fate, at the world.

"My little girl nearly got me into a jam," Stout told me proudly. "As we were leaving La Cloche in a taxi a girl tried to a small bar. An

Argentinian was there. I didn't understand the quarrel, but Yoland smashed a glass in his face. The Madame fought with her too, but she started to scratch the Madame's face. She just came away at the sight of the police. We slipped out a side door."

"It's good you slipped away. That Madame is after her. Probably the police have a silent sympathy for her though, and weren't as bright-eyed as they might be," I said, and asked Yoland her version of the story.

"That dirty sow, Madame Camille, calls me a thief. I decided to show her I wasn't afraid of visiting her place. She was sweet to me, saying that José would pay my bill. I told her José could do it, he meant nothing to me. And he tried to talk to me. Then he sang 'Toreador.' I told him to shut up, but he didn't. *Toreador*," she made her voice nasal and mimicked José's jerky way of singing. "He gave me disgust. He tried to kiss my hand when I was not in the mood, so I struck him with a glass. He bled. He will have scars for weeks."

"She'll kill that Argentinian some day," I said. "He is awful. He gave her syphilis, I think, but he did pay for her treatments afterwards. But she damned near killed him the night she discovered she was sick."

Stout was more sentimental about Yoland than ever now. She confided that he had given her five thousand francs and promised to give her more in the morning when he'd been at the bank. She laughed a warmer rusty chortle now and her clear face was carved above the bluegrey fur on her coat collar. She smiled sphinxly. "He is foolish. He nearly weeps that I don't talk love to him seriously."

When Stout disappeared into the washroom for a few minutes Yoland told another girl of his generosity, and they shrilly shrieked laughter. He was unbelievable to them. Yoland, however, was gentle to Stout when he returned, and they soon left for his hotel.

For six days they were about together. Each day Yoland arrived with a new outfit, a jewelled cigarette case, jewelled vanity box, bracelets, shoes, etc. And Stout continued not only willing but anxious to pay bills for people. Several times when I asked the barman what I owed he told me that Mr. Stout had paid.

At the end of the week Stout departed for America, and I didn't see Yoland for several days. Coming one night into the Dome bar I saw her at the end, seated with Andra, Sporty, and two other *poules*. They were having a hilarious time, and Yoland's voice was higher and more abandoned than usual. It shrieked, but rustily mechanical rather than human. Their jokes could not be heard because of the laughter, in spite of their being loudly spoken.

"Hello Yoland," I greeted her.

Her long lashes went over her grey eyes lizard fashion, and her head swayed towards me, brightly staring, and then it registered in her brain who I was. Whether only drunk, or both doped and drunk, I couldn't judge. She gave an inebriated rasp of laughter, and gasped out, "He wanted my photograph, but see," and showed me a cabinet-sized picture of herself. "He paid two thousand francs for a face that sells on postcards for five sous. He said he would send me money from Canada, whenever I need it. He wants me to write him and he'll have my letters translated. Ha, ha, ha, ha." There was no unkindness in her voice. It was simply ruthlessly unhuman, ironic, unbelieving.

"And he cried at the station, that man. He wished me to marry him but said he understood I wanted freedom. He would wait and if I ever wished I should write him and he would come for me. He is droll. A really sentimental man."

"I guess he finds small-town life doesn't furnish enough exotic excitement," I said.

Andra made a remark that caused the other girls to shriek their shrill hyena laughter again. Yoland's cute crackling ripple sounded more subdued now, because she had laughed too much before at Andra's joke, or because she felt that I might resent their laughing so at a man I'd introduced.

"His pajamas," Andra sputtered, "his beautiful blue pajamas!" She was overcome with mirth and held her hand over her heart.

"They were magnificent, they were blue, but he would not give them to me," Yoland explained, crackling. "I had worn them when I stayed with him. Instead he would give me a necklace, a bracelet, whatever I wished. But the pajamas he would keep, always, without washing, because I had worn them. He liked that I cared for women. He was droll. What a *type!*"

A Death in Paris

Stephen Minot

In their fifties and experienced in the usual sort of emergencies that arise when traveling, Peter and Constance Albright found that they were far from knowledgeable when it came to burying an American citizen in a foreign country.

The fact was that Victor was dead. It was hard to believe. It was even harder to figure out what to do about it.

The arrangements fell to the two of them by sheer chance. They just happened to be in Paris when Victor's coronary hit. Sibi had found him, but she was far too young and inexperienced to handle the details. For the first time the Albrights realized that although Victor's circle of friends was wide, he had never mentioned having relatives anywhere.

What they needed was the assistance of a long-term resident, someone who would know something about French statutes and Parisian ordinances, someone who would advise them with cheerful, good-humored affection. What they needed—more than ever before—was Victor.

But they did manage to cope. They finally roused a Parisian doctor in the middle of the night to make the necessary pronouncements, notified the police, and got Victor a mortuary by dawn. Throughout all this they maintained a cool, dispassionate efficiency. One of the qualities Peter and Constance most admired in each other was the ability to cope. They had gone through financial crises, litigations, and periods of marital alienation without hysteria or loss of dignity. This death, while profoundly upsetting, was a challenge to be dealt with step by step.

When the immediate tasks had been completed they returned to their hotel and waited for the American Embassy to open. Constance took off her suit jacket and lay on her bed without pulling down the spread. Just Peter's height, she was two inches longer than the bed. She lit a cigarette and inhaled deeply. "Too late for a brandy, too early for coffee. An awkward hour. I wish . . ." She paused, inhaled again. "I wish we could just go for a sunrise walk with Victor."

It was the first time they had allowed themselves to say anything personal about Victor. For the length of that long night they had dealt with him only as a problem to be solved.

"It's ironic," Peter said. "The poor guy didn't smoke, never drank too much, never got worked up or tense like the rest of us. It's brutally unfair."

"Did you resent him?"

"Envied him. This life here. The tranquility. Why resent?"

"Because I loved him." She looked at Peter quickly and then stared at the ceiling. "You must have known."

"Everyone loved him." He wasn't sure just how serious a confession this was. Something less, he decided, than actual infidelity. Victor had never seemed to have lovers of either sex. His circle of friends had given him what he needed. Still, Peter didn't feel prepared to press her for details. "Everyone loved him," he said again.

At ten that morning they called the American Embassy. Peter was sure that someone there would handle the paper work. But the woman they dealt with was chilly, detached. The most she would do was to give them names of bureaus and departments that must certify a death, the cause of death, the taxes due, debts owed, the religion of the deceased, and the request for appropriate burial space. It was up to the two of them to do the legwork. What they had first thought would take a morning turned into a three-day struggle with bureaucracy.

One of the problems was that Victor had lived in Paris for well over thirty years without giving up his American citizenship. This in itself was not unheard of but his residency papers were not "in order." They discovered that the man they had known for years as Victor Springdale was—on his long-overdue passport at any rate—

Victor Winters. It was the kind of gently ironic joke he enjoyed. The officials were not amused.

During those three days they wandered from office to office collecting, in Kafkaesque ignorance, an impressive number of documents each of which required signatures, seals, and various stamps. The sheaves were attached rather ineffectively with common pins. It was not until the end of the third day that they finally reached an individual who was, they were assured, authorized to give final approval. Unlike the others, he spoke reasonable English and insisted on it in spite of the fact that Peter's French was passable and Constance's excellent.

"Who, then, is this Victor *Springdale?*" It was a question that had become a refrain.

"We knew him as Victor Springdale," Constance said in French. She found it particularly irritating when waiters or hotel clerks responded to her French with attempts at English. Peter could see a slight reddening of her neck and a tightening of the jaw muscles, signs he knew as danger signals. "We can testify that the two men are the same."

"Two men?"

"One man," Peter said in English. "One man with two different names."

The official, in his traditional dark suit and white shirt, had a striking resemblance to the late Thomas E. Dewey. But then, that was true of many they had met. The man was neither hostile nor stupid, but he was not about to approve without scrutiny a burial and scarce Parisian cemetery space for a foreign national whose papers were not in order. "You've known Mr.—ah, the deceased for some time now?"

"Over twenty years," Constance said, still speaking French. By now her determination not to speak English had become a subtle signal of hostility that was quite clear to both men.

"Twenty-one to be exact," Peter said in English, to be cooperative. They would be in here all day if Constance really got her back up.

"It is cause for surprise," the official said, softly, as if musing aloud, tapping his pencil on the desk top, "that such close friends—

friends over so long a span—would be unsure about the name of the deceased and . . ." he shuffled through the papers, "his religion and . . ." tap-tap ". . . even his source of income?"

Indeed, it was cause for surprise. Even astonishment. They had assumed that Victor was a fairly successful fashion photographer who had been lucky enough to have lived on the Left Bank for decades. Yet there was no record of his ever having paid any taxes under either name. He hadn't even registered as a foreign national. It was true that he rarely talked about his past and almost never about money, but that was part of his nature. Modest, gentle, and generous, those were his qualities. With his round face and easy smile, he invited trust from everyone. He had a quiet talent for bringing others together and making them feel at home without ever asserting himself.

They had met Victor on their first trip to Paris some twenty years earlier. After that, neither of them were quite sure whether it was their friendship with him or their fondness for his little group that brought them back almost every spring. Since Victor enjoyed entertaining at home, they had come to know his large studio apartment as well as any in New York. It was spacious, but the section they used the most was in front by the French windows. During the day one could look out on the Rue de Fleurus, just one block from the Luxembourg Gardens. At night, of course, the shutters were closed and the large, scarred, round table served as the focal point. It was around this table that they shared their aperitif, the long, leisurely meal, and the endless talk. Since the stove, sink, and tiny refrigerator were simply lined up along the side wall, there was really no reason to use the rest of the room.

In the background, however, in the darkened interior, was his studio space—two ancient cameras, the bellows type permanently mounted on heavy mahogany tripods, dusty lamps with enormous bulbs, reflecting screens. On the walls one could barely make out fashion shots, some framed and some not, many inscribed. Unlike many Americans, Victor never bored his friends with talk about his professional activities. He was much more concerned with the arts, politics, and the special interests of his guests.

Peter had always envied Victor's gentle, uncharged life. It was a sharp contrast with the pace Peter and Constance had to maintain in New York. Their apartment was in the East Seventies, but Peter spent much of his time—including most Saturdays—at his architectural office on West Tenth Street. He and his two partners took on more work than many larger firms. Constance was equally involved with her job as magazine editor, heading a small publication for women executives. It seemed to Peter that the two of them spent an inordinate number of days in the workplace and too many of their evenings entertaining clients. The only time they could really let go of obligations and be themselves was with their friends in Paris. It was surprising really, how often that phrase came up—"our friends in Paris."

When the man who looked like Dewey finally approved their collection of documents with his signature, Peter and Constance were too tired to celebrate. They had a quiet dinner and went directly back to their hotel room. "I could hardly believe it," Constance said. "After three days, that fussy *petit fonctionnaire* finally gives us a date and a place. Just like that." She took off her shoes and massaged her feet. "Is there anything we've forgotten?"

"What about announcements? I suppose it's possible that we'll be the only ones at the burial."

"Only us? God, Peter, that's hardly a decent funeral—even for an agnostic. If that's what he was."

"And Sibi, of course."

"Of course And that mother of hers. Gladys? Gladys Kruger. I'll call them in the morning. I'm really not up to it now. But I keep feeling that Victor should have a big group. One last party."

"How easy it would be in New York, an announcement in the *Times* and maybe just a few phone calls. But here . . . ."

The problem was that while Victor Springdale was one of the most sociable people they knew, his friends were scattered and transitory. A few were models, but he could hardly be described as "in" the fashion set. There were some Americans, like Peter and Constance, but there were just as many English and Continental friends. Some were in the professions, others in business, a few in the arts. He was catholic in his friendships. But because they were from all over, they came and went like migratory birds. They were not likely to read obituary columns.

Peter stripped to his undershorts and put on a bathrobe. Then he wiped out the two hotel glasses and mixed identical drinks, a double shot of Scotch and a splash of water in each. But he left them on the bureau, caught up in his own thoughts. "We've got to get some of the group there," he said almost to himself. "It wouldn't be right not to . . . ." He went to the window and looked out at the darkened city, but that was a mistake. Seeing the deserted street made him think of Victor dying alone. For the first time he felt a chilling melancholy sweep over him. It was an unnerving sensation, almost like fear. There had been times, always at night, alone, battling insomnia when he had felt this kind of isolation and futility. He turned back to Constance and said with forced energy, "Get a pencil. It's time to make a list of our Paris friends."

Constance, still dressed but with her shoes off, sat in the only chair, a sheet of paper spread on a Paris phone book in her lap. They both had a predilection for making lists. Peter handed her a drink, sipped his own, and sat opposite her on the edge of the bed. In this manner they began to reconstruct the most recent evening at Victor's, the last social gathering before his coronary. Names were not enough; they had to figure out ways of locating those transient friends. As Peter's drink began to smooth out the tensions of the day, fragments of the evening returned to him as if on videotape.

There had been eight—no, seven guests plus Victor sitting around that table, an echo of countless other evenings in that studio. The faces sometimes changed, but there was always a mood of relaxed intimacy. On this night there was only one couple Peter and Constance remembered clearly from other years. The rest were vaguely familiar. Yet by the end of the aperitif they were all knit together as members of Victor's circle—Victor's little family.

"We do depend on you," the overweight Italian said to Victor. Enrico was what everyone called him, but what was the last name? Torelli? Yes, Torelli. He kept insisting that Italy depended on the United States, smiling, gesturing widely, but playing particularly to the Americans. "We Italians inch our way toward anarchy. You have no idea. Our national preoccupation. Kidnappings no longer make headlines. They are like car thefts. And now they are holding art objects for ransom."

"Kidnapping a painting?" Sibi Kruger said. "A *painting?*"

Sibi, a young, aspiring model from Dubuque, was easily astonished. She and her mother had arrived with Enrico, though it was not clear yet which, if either, was intimate with him.

"Paintings, sculptures. Anything of value. The only solution is to sell everything of value to America! Everything. You hold them for us. The Pieta? I can get it for you cheap. Certainly. Or the Forum. Perhaps you could set it up on the prairie next to your London Bridge. For the sake of safety, everything must be shipped to America!" And then with an apparent inborn courtesy he gestured to Carleton Fitzwilliam. "And Great Britain, of course."

"On credit, I trust." Carleton was a wine importer from London. He and his "special friend," Chantal, were regulars, though she lived in Brussels. "No room for the Forum, I'm afraid. But all the little stuff. Statuary, Etruscan pottery, anything that hasn't already been smuggled out."

"'Smuggled out'? You hear what happened to us at Pompeii?" Gladys Kruger said, laughing, jangling her collection of bracelets. Lean and bony, she advertised herself with oversized jewelry. "Sibi and I picked up a piece of pottery no bigger than a dime just for a keepsake and you know, they held us all night in that crummy jail and even then I had to wire home for money to pay the fine and get out of there. You can't get away with a thing in Pompeii."

"Ah, what a shame you didn't know me then," Enrico said, beaming. "One call and I would have had you out of there. Just one call and the district capitano would have given you his profound apology. In writing. It is true."

"But I *told* Ma it was against the law," Sibi said. She had the unmistakable look of a model, tall with blond hair stylishly trimmed short; but her voice was adolescent and still Iowa. "There were zillions of signs saying it was against the law."

"Don't you worry," Enrico said, "I have some gemmy little pieces from Pompeii I could let you have at, as they say, a *prix d'ami.*"

"Enrico is a veritable storehouse," Victor said gently. "Depend on him. By the way, next time you're in Rome, he could serve as your guide too." Enrico nodded. "He would be happy to show you about and keep you out of trouble. He has more influence than the pope himself. It's always good to have a friend in a foreign city. And here in Paris, of course, I'm at your disposal. I'm no pope, but I do have a few contacts."

"Dear Victor," Chantal Thibault said. Her languid charm made women like Mrs. Kruger seem angular and crass. "How long has it been, Victor, five, perhaps seven years?" And to the others, "If it were not for Victor, Carleton and I would scarcely be able to see each other."

It was not at all clear to Peter why that might be true, but it was unmistakably more than a kindly exaggeration. She was not the type to say anything she didn't mean.

Victor merely smiled and shrugged. He didn't like having the conversation turned to him. Instead, he began asking Gladys Kruger and her daughter which fashion houses they had applied to so far and suggesting others they should now consider. He also advised her about which were the better restaurants in the area, but Mrs. Kruger was far more interested in her daughter's career than she was in French cuisine. She explained to them all why it was that someone with Sibi's statuesque build would be far more appreciated in Paris than New York. This struck Peter as naive, even absurd. But Victor was, as always, quietly supportive.

"You just might be right," he said. "And you clearly have the perseverance—both of you. That's really what it takes—good looks and a lot of perseverance. And friends."

Peter found it astonishing, this soothing optimism. He himself would have warned both mother and daughter that they were walking into a world where outsiders weren't wanted, where not knowing the language perfectly was risky, and where the pay scales were far lower than in New York. Trying to break into the Parisian fashion world would be a bare-fisted fight. Shouldn't someone warn them? But Victor had the ability to make life seem like a musical comedy, and who was Peter to break the illusion?

It was clear that Mrs. Kruger and daughter had much to learn from Victor, but it was not at all as clear why someone like Chantal Thibault would feel so grateful. In addition to her native French, she spoke perfect English with an Oxbridge accent and occasionally shared some wry comment in Italian with Enrico. As for her lover, Carleton Fitzwilliam, his dealings with vintners made him an expert Francophile. Yet for all their apparent sophistication, the two of them treated Victor as their benefactor.

"I have a treat for you two," Victor said, turning to Peter and Constance. "As I remember it, you were about the first Americans in the Pompidou. . . ."

"Thanks to you," Peter said.

"Well, here's another delight for you. The refurbished Giverny. They've done it just right. A real gem. It's a little complicated finding it, but I know a driver, a very good driver, who will take you there for less than train fare. He is not, shall we say, fully licensed, but he will take you there as, well, a paying friend."

It was typical of Victor's arrangements. Somehow he always knew about guides without licenses, restaurants that had just opened or had just moved up from two stars to three, art exhibits that had scarcely been advertised. Such information was particularly surprising in view of the fact that even after thirty-five years in Paris Victor's French was still terrible.

He must have been able to read and understand French fairly well in order to be so informed, but as a speaker, his accent was atrocious. In anyone else, Peter and Constance would have found this arrogant. But Victor being Victor, they excused it as a quirky stubbornness. Besides, it was this very eccentricity that had resulted in their meeting Victor two decades earlier.

They had been on Boulevard Montparnasse, looking for an agreeable restaurant when they had seen a slightly plump American in the grip of an irate cabdriver. The cabby was speaking French so fast that even Peter could not make it out. Constance, however, managed to pick up the drift and interrupted sharply. Somehow she managed to calm everyone, that is, placated the cabdriver and dispersed the crowd. The victim was not even ruffled.

Peter, feeling compassion for anyone trying to deal with a cabby without knowing French, ended up paying the fare. After introductions they asked this Victor Springdale if he could recommend a good restaurant in the area. Surprisingly, he could. It was an establishment that had just acquired a masterful chef who had quit his previous job with a four-star restaurant on the Right Bank when he discovered that the owner was not French but in fact a Romanian living illegally in France under an assumed name. Victor urged them to try it for lunch—that being the hour. But he himself would not be able to join them. He had just been down to the Algerian district to exchange foreign currency for francs and had apparently lost his wallet to a pickpocket. He hadn't discovered the theft until he tried to pay the cabdriver. Naturally, Peter invited him to be their guest.

Victor, it turned out, was an expert in French cuisine and felt a deep reverence for French wines—a passion shared by Constance. The two of them got along beautifully from the start. When Victor discovered that Peter was an architect, he proved to be highly knowledgeable about what Paris had to offer. He took them on lengthy walking tours of the city, serving as a relaxed and enthusiastic guide. Peter, who until then tended to view foreign travel as more of a challenge than a pleasure, felt at ease for the first time since coming abroad.

Victor, they learned, had remained in Paris after his wartime service as a photographer in the U.S. Army. There seemed to have been a woman involved, but she was no longer on the scene. "Actually it was French cooking that kept me here," Victor said, smiling and polishing his round glasses. "That and a number of good friends."

On their last full day in Paris, Peter and Constance decided to invite him out again. Predictably, they had become increasingly edgy with each other. Enforced intimacy always put them both off. Victor was delighted to hear from them, but on that particular evening he was having some friends in for a winetasting. He regretted that he had no time for shopping, but if Peter and Constance would be willing to buy some groceries, he would expand the wine tasting into a respectable five-course meal and turn a simple little gathering into something a bit more special.

After so many tedious meals by themselves with the inevitable waiting for service, this sounded like a refreshing change. They were able to buy almost everything he had suggested and a good deal more just out of gratitude. What they spent was still less than an evening out in New York would have been.

There were ten, perhaps fifteen people there, a vivid and lively assemblage. Sharing the wine tasting and then the preparation of the meal generated a true *esprit*. Almost from the start Peter lost the sense of being a foreigner, an outsider—a sensation that tended to spoil his vacation travels. Here he was enveloped in the comfortable sense of membership in this lively and varied group. And so, apparently, did Constance. Back in New York they found themselves describing the trip as their best, focusing on that single evening.

The phone rang. It jolted them back to the present. Absurdly, they looked at each other as if one of them should know who on earth would be calling their hotel room at 10:30 at night.

Peter answered and heard a hoarse, faint whisper: "Peter? Peter Albright? Are you awake?" He managed to identify the speaker as Sibi, the model from Iowa, though she seemed to have her hand cupped around the mouthpiece. "Look, could I see you?"

He felt a flash of annoyance. He was tired and in no mood for mysteries. "Anything wrong?"

"Five minutes. Will you still be up?"

"Of course."

He hung up and repeated the conversation to Constance.

"Must be important," she said. "Do you suppose the girl has some information we don't?"

"Not likely. We knew him better."

"Still, she was the one who found him. Maybe she was having an affair with him."

"With Victor?" He shook his head. Victor didn't seem the type. Besides, Peter had always thought of their Paris friends as a harmonious and open group—not one with secrets.

"It's true Sibi had a key, but he gives . . . gave keys to everyone."

Victor's building had originally been managed by a concierge, but in the late 60s she had gone the way of British nannies. As a result, guests could ring individual apartments, but it was up to each apartment owner to trudge down and unlock the front door. Since Victor lived on the third floor, he simply gave out keys not only for the front door but for his apartment as well. For a number of years Peter assumed that he was a privileged friend. It was disappointing to discover how generous Victor was with his keys.

So it was not at all surprising that Sibi had been able to let herself in on the evening he had planned to show her the new publicity shots. The original photographs, taken only a month before, were of no use because her mother had insisted that Sibi have her hair cut shorter. But when Sibi went up to his apartment to see the new prints, he was sprawled on the floor, his filet and an assortment of groceries scattered in front of him. He had evidently just entered the apartment after the three-floor climb when his heart gave out.

Peter had never thought much of Sibi, but he had to admit that her response was very much to her credit. She rolled him over and gave him CPR just as she had learned in high school back in Dubuque. When that failed, she called Peter and Constance, asking them to locate a doctor and an ambulance, though she was quite sure Victor was dead. She had not called her mother because, as she explained, "Ma would go bananas."

That was four nights ago. It seemed to Peter more like a month. What they had hoped would be another relaxing vacation had become even more tense and complicated than their working lives.

When Sibi knocked at their hotel door, she was out of breath. "I didn't want to wake the night clerk," she explained. "So I had to climb the stupid stairs. Sometimes they won't let girls visit at night. Frenchmen they really think dirty."

"What's up?" Peter asked.

"Sorry to make it so late, but I had to wait until Ma went to sleep. She means well, but there's a lot of things she just can't handle, you know?"

"I hope it's nothing serious," Constance said.

"Well, it is. Really. But it's my own stupid fault. I should have thought of this when I found him."

"Victor?"

"Yeah, but it was a weird time, you know? I mean, here is this dead man. . . ."

"It must have been a shock," Constance said.

"You'd think I'd remember what I came for. After I called you I just went back to our hotel. Like a dope, I completely forgot what I'd come for."

"What you came for?"

"The glossies. My photos. He had a bunch of them. With the new hairdo? And instead of looking around for them, I just cleared out of there. I told Ma yesterday she should go up and get them, but she says there's probably some French law against going in a dead man's apartment. She's scared stiff of getting arrested again. I mean, she was sure we were both going to get raped that time in Pompeii. Rape is big with her. Anyhow, she won't go anywhere near the apartment, and she even made me throw the key in the river like in the movies. She says she doesn't want to be caught with it. I swear, she can get real spacey."

With a growing sense of uneasiness, Peter began to see that he was being asked to go up to Victor's apartment with Sibi and locate the prints before the authorities cleared the place out and did whatever they normally do with the property of individuals without heirs.

"At night?" Peter asked. "You want to go over at night?"

"What's wrong?" Then, wide-eyed, "Victor's not still up there, is he?"

"Of course not. It's just that—well, why not during the day?"

"Ma would kill me if she found out I was going. But if we actually got them—well, she'd just sputter. Right now she's out cold. She sleeps like an ox."

"Well, maybe I could go by myself tomorrow."

"Oh, Peter, you'd never find them. He's got a zillion of them. But I know just where mine would be. Besides, I hear they sometimes seal the place up to keep people from going back in. They could do that in the morning and then what would I do? Look, it won't take us more than a minute, really."

Peter sighed. "Oh I suppose."

She sprang out of her chair with a motion more like a cheerleader than a model and gave Peter a quick but firm kiss on the lips. Then she grabbed both his hands and helped him up from where he was sitting on the bed. It was a schoolgirl's gesture, but he caught a quick glimpse of Constance. The tendons beneath her jaw were tight. "We'll all go," she said. "Peter's French is not as dazzling as he likes to think, and you never can tell what you might run into."

Their hotel was less than a five-minute walk from Victor's apartment. That was hardly accidental. Being in Paris meant seeing a good deal of Victor, so they had kept returning to the same neighborhood.

The route was so familiar that for a moment it seemed as if the three of them were planning to pick Victor up and go to a cafe for a cognac and talk. Perhaps others would join them and the conversation would flow easily, guided by Victor's quiet good cheer. Victor never was bothered by the professional anxieties that plagued Peter and most of his friends in New York. Victor never complained about inflation, student riots, terrorist bombings. "Victor's my guru," Peter used to say with a laugh, though the two of them never discussed anything deep.

But that was all gone now. The reality of it washed back on him once again with alarming force. Somehow he'd been betrayed and abandoned.

The climb up the three flights of stairs was dreamlike. The single dim bulb on each landing was on a timer and stayed lit just long enough for them to reach the next switch. Those clicks and their breathing were the only sounds. The air was dank and musty.

They reached Victor's landing just as the light snapped off again. Constance started to grope for the switch, but Peter said there was no need. "I could find this lock blindfolded," he muttered.

It did take some scratching about, however, and when the door finally swung open he pushed it too hard in his nervousness and it swung back against the wall.

"Who the bloody hell is that?" a voice bellowed.

Peter stepped back as if he had been hit, and from behind him Constance shoved forward. Speaking French in her most managerial voice she said. "What are you doing here? We are going to call the police."

The light flashed on and they all squinted. There, on Victor's large sofa bed, was a couple. They were sitting up, both of them, she holding the covers up to her throat.

"How did you get in?" the man said. Just as Peter recognized Carleton Fitzwilliam, Carleton added, "Well, for godsake don't stand in the door. Come in and close it, will you?"

Sibi gasped. "Weird," she said.

"Not half as weird as having you pop in like this," Carleton said.

"If you're going to stay," Chantal said in her most gracious voice, "would you mind turning about for a few minutes? We're not exactly dressed for company."

Peter, Constance, and Sibi turned and faced the door. They could hear the other two padding about, locating clothes. "This strikes me as positively morbid," Constance said. "Surely you've heard about poor Victor?"

"We heard," Carleton said. "Terrible shock."

"Wednesdays are our day to borrow the place," Chantal said. "It's been a tradition of sorts whenever we're in town. Victor would have approved—one last time."

"Goodness," Sibi said. "What on earth for?" And then, flustered, she added, "I mean, why not hotels?"

"Hotels require passports."

"So what?" Peter said, indignant for Victor's sake. "No Parisian hotel is going to give you a hard time about that."

"It is not the hotel that would object," Chantal said. "They merely record the facts. But I would prefer not to have my name on the books. I am married, you see, and my husband is a very harsh man."

"Victor understands," Carleton said. "Understood, that is. And we've always made it up to him. All the wine you've enjoyed here is from my account."

"Victor did that once for us too," Constance said, her voice still resonating disapproval. "He let us sleep here when our hotel reservations were fouled up. He said he'd stay with friends."

"Of course," Carleton said.

"Well, he didn't. An acquaintance of ours saw him sitting in the Gare du Nord at six in the morning. He was unshaved. He'd been there all night."

"Good Lord," Chantal said, "do you suppose all those times..?"

"We're proper now," Carleton said. The three by the door turned around. Carleton and Chantal looked as if they were ready for another one of Victor's informal dinners, but Carleton's face was dark as it never had been when Victor was alive. "Now what is all this about?—all of you barging in here in the middle of the night."

"It's kind of my fault," Sibi said, opening wide architectural drawers one after another, her back to them. "I'm awfully sorry," she muttered. The drawers were stuffed with photographs, many of them curling. "He took a new batch of glossies. With my new hair style. You like it?"

"Your hair?" Carleton asked. "At this hour?"

"Oh, wow, here they are." She started looking them over, one at a time, cocking her head to one side. "Nice. Really nice. I mean, I couldn't even submit new resumes without these."

"I could have recommended other photographers," Chantal said. "Ones that are better known."

Sibi lowered the prints, letting them hang there at her side. Standing there in the dark recesses of that room without makeup she looked gawky and unsure. "The thing is, we don't have the money. We're practically flat-out broke as it is. We wouldn't even have come abroad at all if we hadn't been introduced to Victor by letter—someone we knew from back home who's over here now driving rich Americans around Paris. He told us how Victor would help. For nothing—sort of."

"You mean," Constance said, "Victor took all those photographs without charging a fee?"

"Well, he's not a professional photographer, you know. Just kind of a hobby. He got all this stuff after the war . . . ." She gestured to the old cameras and lights. "With what the army gives you when you get out. But he never could make a living out of it. I mean, he doesn't even know much French, you know."

"No professional work?" Peter said. "How on earth did he get along?"

Sibi shrugged. "Not very well, really. Ma takes . . . took him out to little restaurants a lot. Sometimes he seemed kind of hungry. That's all we could do for him. And he was so kind to us."

"Hungry?" Constance said. "That's absurd. He was always entertaining."

"Only when someone like you guys bought the groceries. What you left on your plates, he scraped into jars. I used to help him. He said he fed stray cats at the Luxembourg. That's what he said. Of course whoever ate here then owed him a meal."

Carleton shook his head. "He must have had some money. What about the rent?"

"Mr. Torelli—you remember him? He sneaks things out of Italy and sells them to Americans he meets here at Victor's. So he paid it. With a little extra now and then."

"Paid his rent?" Carleton said. "In exchange for contacts? What a bloody fraud!"

"Fraud!" Constance said. "You and your wine so you could use his bed. And poor Victor spending nights huddled in a train station."

"My wine, but you two bought the groceries for all those gatherings. You Americans and your foreign aid. What were you buying? I assume you were getting something in return."

"Nothing sordid like a bed." The tendons of her jaw muscles were like cords. "Peter," she said, turning to him, "what's happened? I thought we were among friends. A lovely circle of friends."

"It's death," Chantal said softly. "Death does that."

"Don't be morbid," Carleton said. "It lifts a veil, death does. Haven't you noticed?"

Peter looked around and saw that they were all suddenly strangers. They would never meet again. How could everything have come unglued so quickly?

"It has nothing to do with death," Carleton said. "The simple fact is that our friend Victor whom we trusted—was playing what you Americans so charmingly call a confidence game."

"Playing a confidence game?" Chantal said with a touch of a smile. "Dear Victor wasn't the only one."

Carmencita

Waverley Root

Back in the early twenties, the uninhibited and unrepressed souls who made up the Paris edition of the *Chicago Tribune* gathered nightly in a dark and dirty *bistro* on the Rue Lamartine. There, across the street from the newspaper office, editorial workers and proofreaders, with an occasional stray from the business offices, met every evening for dinner, bringing with them the girls of their temporary choice. None of these young men had yet reached the point of marrying. Few had even acquired *petites amies;* those who had, owed that situation to the determination of the ladies rather than to any constancy of their own.

There was thus a heavy turnover in the feminine population of the *bistro,* or what might be termed a constant internal redistribution. To put it more bluntly, when one of the boys tired of Gaby or Elvire or Vivienne, another was very likely to inherit her. But sooner or later even those young ladies who enjoyed widespread popularity drifted away. The affairs that began there were strictly ephemeral.

Against this background, it required a considerable amount of amorous diligence for any one person to stand out. By common consent, nevertheless, Ray Farquharson did. The accolade was awarded him on no vulgar quantitative basis. After all, the sports editor had managed for a number of years to pick up a different girl every evening. Farquharson's distinction was qualitative. For him each new affair was the one great love of his life. The average duration of his amours was about a fortnight, but while they lasted they were, every one of them, unparalleled passions.

In the throes of love, Farquharson was a man without memory. If during one of his hymns of praise to the current favorite he was reminded of similar words uttered a week earlier in praise of another, he dismissed the earlier with an offhand reference to puppy love. If you persisted in skepticism, he became really angry with the righteous anger of the lover who is devoted unto death and resents the scoffing of baser souls.

Farquharson was older than most of his colleagues and the only one who, in that early period, was married. But his marriage weighed lightly upon him. Familiarity had finished by breeding not so much contempt as indifference. The current marriage was either his fourth or his sixth, the difficulty in assigning it a number resting in his own haziness as to which of the previous liaisons had been dignified by public authority. All except his last marriage took place in the United States. The final episode had been Parisian.

It was probably just as well that Farquharson had left America for a country where breach of promise suits were rare, where alimony was less easy to secure, and where neither public opinion nor police authority was ordinarily exerted to curb amorous exuberance. One theory current in the office was, indeed, that Farquharson had originally come to Paris for the sake of these advantages. The story ran that his ever-increasing obligations to pay alimony had finally outrun his income.

It was no secret that his French marriage had long since lost its savor, first for himself and, soon thereafter, for his wife. His reason for maintaining the fiction that he was married he explained by saying, during a lucid interval between affairs, "What's the sense of being divorced? As long as I have one wife, I can't get hooked by another."

The marital establishment also came in handy as a place in which to live between periods of sharing apartments with his successive girls. Setting up house with them was a measure of his sincerity, of his own belief in the genuineness of each new love. He was not only willing to try housekeeping with each new inamorata, but even willing, though chronically penniless and therefore seldom able, to pay for the necessary equipment. Unfortunately the bills usually continued to come in after the idyll had ended.

Carmencita

There was one occasion on which Farquharson only barely escaped having his marriage legally dissolved, and another union from which he would have found it difficult to slip out, fastened on him. On that occasion he made the mistake of becoming enamored of a young lady many cuts above his usual taste, one of a species rare in the Paris of that date, a woman lawyer. She was one of the few for whom he established a joint apartment, although in this instance, to be exact, the lady footed most of the bills. And this time his customary protestations of a desire for a divorce fell on the ears of someone capable of doing something about it The woman advocate was well on the way to freeing, and re-caging, him before the affair ended.

It was a near thing, for Farquharson's plans had become so definite that a date had been set at which he was to be introduced to the young lady's innumerable and strictly old-fashioned relatives at a formal dinner. It was probably dread of this ordeal which caused Farquharson, no very sober individual at best, to overindulge to such an extent that he wound up in a suburban railroad coach at almost the exact hour set for the dinner. Stumbling out of the tram at the next stop, he telephoned his intended that he had just discovered he was in Versailles and would be a trifle late for dinner. On leaving the phone booth, he realized that he was actually in St. Germaine-en-laye. This so unnerved him that he never got to the dinner at all.

Undiscouraged, the girl covered up for him by telling her family a story of sudden illness, which they pretended to believe. The dread of marrying irrevocably into an orthodox French family probably also accounted for the sudden cooling of Farquharson's affections and his abrupt departure. A wandering American promoter had turned up in Paris as shepherd of a dance marathon, which had just proved a resounding flop in France. Anxious to try Spain, he engaged Farquharson as publicity man, and Farquharson, quitting the paper briefly, took off for San Sebastian, leaving with only an abbreviated note to the sharer of his home.

A few of the wanderer's artful love letters came through, but at increasingly greater intervals, and finally ceased altogether. Fighting the realization that she had been jilted, the girl appealed to Jim

Plant, the news editor of the paper, to write to Farquharson. But before he had time to write, Plant received a letter from Farquharson. It appeared that the rover had met in Spain the great passion of his life, the one woman to whom he could cleave until death did them part. This, at last, was the real thing! The reason for the letter itself was a request that Plant do a little job of amatory arson and burn Farquharson's bridges behind him—in short, break the news that the Paris affair was over.

Plant had little taste for the assignment, but he finally called at the lady's apartment—formerly hers and Farquharson's—and broke the news as delicately as he could. There were, as he had anticipated and feared, tears. Never a man able to resist feminine weeping, Plant found himself lending the girl enough money to go to Spain to win Farquharson back. But a little later in the evening he also found himself consoling her in the classic fashion. The project for a trip to Spain somehow lapsed. The lady lawyer did not offer to return the loan, but Farquharson's ex-apartment came in handy, and considering one thing and another, Plant did not regret the outlay.

Meanwhile, it had not taken long for the American promoter to discover that Spain agreed with France about dance marathons. Farquharson, after previously wiring for (a) his old job back, and (b) a sufficient advance to pay his fare, returned to Paris. For a time, curiously enough, he exhibited a certain coldness towards Plant, who, he seemed to feel, had somehow done him out of something.

But he did not return alone. He had brought back the great Iberian passion.

She was preceded by samples of Farquharson's pressagentry which made it clear why he had been picked for the job of trying to persuade Spaniards to abandon bullfights for dance marathons. The girl was, Farquharson explained, a member of one of the most aristocratic families of Spain. The details of the story were vague, but one gathered that courting her had involved running the gauntlet of a host of duennas. The couple's departure had involved not so much an elopement as an abduction. Farquharson was not sure that the police weren't looking for him in Spain; he was certain the girl's brothers were.

The girl, when Farquharson's colleagues finally got a look at her did not appear to live up to the advance billing. If one could overlook the fact that she was more than a trifle over-padded, one might have called her voluptuous. She might have been considered the baby-face type had it not been for her make-up, which in thickness was more likely to remind one of a Van Gogh than a baby. The rouge was brilliant, the lipstick was a wild-colored crust, and a question-mark of jet black hair lay coiled on her forehead, to which it was apparently glued.

The most alarming feature about her, however, was her eyes. The lids of these were weighted down with a coating of green paint so thick that merely looking at them fatigued the average beholder. The brows were imbedded in mascara, and each separate eyelash was so thickly embalmed in the same substance that there was a minute bead at the tip of each. The general effect was that of an actress about to appear in a stadium seating 40,000 persons.

Her name, inevitably, was Carmen.

Her appearance invoked a variety of skeptical comment concerning Farquharson's account of her origin. To all these he retorted heatedly, adding details of her exalted lineage. Knowing that none of his colleagues had been to Spain, he maintained that the heavy use of cosmetics was normal among pillars of society there, and attributed all slurs on Carmen's gentility to her critics' ignorance of Spanish standards.

Firsthand bulletins on the habits of Carmen, all unfavorable, were soon available, for Farquharson, with what may have been either *jemenfoutisme* or malice, established himself with his Carmencita in a hotel room just across the courtyard from another he had occupied, three romances back, with a member of the editorial staff, Edna Keen. Edna was still living there. As neither Carmen nor Farquharson ever appeared to discover that their windows were provided with shades, Farquharson's ex-favorite could provide a blow-by-blow account of the Carmen-Farquharson romance—which she did with relish.

Blow-by-blow seemed to be an exact description, for almost all of the private contacts of the couple were of a belligerent kind. The fortunate occupants of rooms whose windows were located at the proper angle across the court enjoyed almost daily the sight of a display of Spanish temper accompanied by the crash of crockery. From the stage of throwing (on Carmen's part) and dodging (on Farquharson's), the pair progressed regularly to in-fighting, in which Carmen used all the weapons with which nature had endowed her—principally nails and teeth. This phase of the combat ended ordinarily with Carmen reduced to immobility by being pinned down on the bed by Farquharson's slightly greater weight. This was not the final stage of such encounters, but it is the last which may be set down here.

A little later the two could be seen moving about again. Farquharson applying court-plaster to his face and Carmen restoring her make-up. Occasionally the tranquil and contented strains of a languid Spanish song would float from the open window.

Compared with the accounts of these set-tos, the more routine details of Carmen's life held less savor. The office knew, from its conscientious observer on the spot, that Carmen's life followed a regular pattern of sleep, applying make-up, fighting Farquharson, succumbing to him, restoring make-up, emerging briefly for dinner, and returning to sleep again. It realized that this was a full day, for it had been informed that in preparing her beauty for the outer world, Carmen devoted a full hour to each eye alone. But such items were greeted with not quite so much interest as were the accounts of the battles royal between Farquharson and his Castilian aristocrat.

When he arrived at work bearing the scars of honorable combat, Farquharson was wonderful fun to bait. One day he arrived with a sizable section of his cheek raked open by Carmen's nails. This rowelling had missed his left eye by not more than an eighth of an inch. Unabashed by the closeness of Farquharson's escape from becoming a one-eyed lover, the boys pounced upon him and the witticisms flew thick and fast.

"Goddamn it!" Farquharson shouted at last. "What do you fellows know about love? None of you ever had a woman who loved you enough to scrape half your face off."

In calmer moments, he would exhibit his wounds complacently, even boasting about the fierceness of the Spanish temperament, a fury which, he implied, was active in love as well as in combat. In this he was backed by Carmen, who explained to Edna Keen in one the few English sentences she ever managed to utter: "In Spain, no fight, no love."

She did not get even this far in French. In spite of having managed to pick up a few English phrases, mostly obscene, from Farquharson, she never succeeded in getting anywhere at all with French. Even Edna, who had no reason to love her and, indeed, did not, once took pity on what she decided must be her lonesome and boring existence, and went to the trouble of buying her a Spanish novel.

Carmen responded queerly to the gift, failing even to thank Edna for it. Edna ascribed this to the absence of any common language, and thought no more of it. That is, she thought no more of it until the day when she found herself entertaining a friend who spoke Spanish. Feeling that it would relieve Carmen's loneliness if she could meet someone who knew her language, Edna suggested that they visit the Spanish girl. When they entered Carmen's room, they found her seated before her dressing table, about to start work on her second eye.

Very quickly the two girls exhausted the ordinary subjects of conversation. Falling back desperately on the first thought that came into her head Edna asked her friend to inquire how Carmen had liked the book she had given her. Carmen hesitated for a moment. Then she replied in a voice pitched far below her usual strident tones. The interpreter relayed her information to Edna in a tone of surprise: "She says she can't read."

"What?" Edna cried. "Can't read? What does she mean?"

"She doesn't know how," the interpreter explained. "She never learned to read or write. She says she comes from a very poor family. She never went to school."

"So *that's* his aristocratic lady love!" Edna exploded. "So *that's* what he sneaked away from a duenna! . . . No! There's something wrong. It can't be! I know she gets letters from home and answers them. Ask her how she does that if she can't read or write."

The interpreter asked the questions and then explained: "She goes to the Berlitz School. When she gets a letter, she takes it there.

They read it to her and she dictates the answer."

Carmen spoke up again. The interpreter listened and then said: "She says she has one now. She doesn't want to take it there because the last time she was ashamed. She wants to know if I will read it to her. Should I?"

"Oh, boy!" Edna exulted. "Should you? I wouldn't miss it for worlds!"

The letter was from Carmen's family. It bewailed the fact that señor Farquharson, who had made such generous promises when he was in San Sebastian four months ago, was now three months behind on the forty pesetas per month he had promised them in exchange for the companionship of Carmencita. If he could not pay, would he not at least send her back, so that she might again help support her large family?

With whoops of glee, Edna broke into the office half an hour later to blast forever the fable of Carmen's noble birth. Since Farquharson was broke, as always, the staff raised the money to ship her back to Spain and also to pay off, along with a little interest, the arrears in the rent charged for her person.

Farquharson was not angry at this intervention in his personal affairs. He had just become interested in a dancer at the Moulin Rouge. This time it was the real thing.

The #63 Bus from the Gare de Lyon

Daniel Stern

Paul and Letty Gerard had never been to the Père Lachaise cemetery. They'd been to Paris a hundred times—okay, maybe a dozen, once for six months, the enormous fifth floor apartment near the Parc Royale. All enough to make them feel that classic American sense of owning the city: *our town*, less sentimental than *our song* but the similar possessive—comfortable walking in the Marias, the outdoor food stands on the Rue de Rivoli, easy in the changes in the Metro, familiar with the benches near the fountain in the Place de Vosges, knowing the numbers of the bus to L'Opera or Saint Germaine des Pres. But they'd never made time for the famous cemetery where Oscar Wilde was buried, Balzac, Colette, who Letty particularly loved—and the family joke, Paul's literary ancestor, his doppelgänger, the nineteenth-century writer Paul Gerard.

Naturally, Paris was the place for the second honeymoon, though the whole notion wasn't Paul's or Letty's. It was the kids' idea, not the first time the young out-romanticized the parents. Some *kids*, Sarah the accountant and Gabriel the poet-screenwriter, easily forty-five years between them. One was twenty-two, one twenty-three.

"Do you mind the convention, the cliché?" Paul asked her. "First honeymoons are problematic enough."

"We can finally go see Père Lachaise," Letty said. "See where your namesake is buried." She grinned in her easy way at him. Paul was the solemn one, Letty lighter-than-air, at least that was the mythology of their twenty-five-year marriage, begun right after graduation from Cornell.

"I think my grandfather's real name was Gerovsky," he said.

"French immigration just got very creative. Though it's nice to have such a fancy figure behind me."

Paul Gerard had been a minor literary figure, a friend of Balzac's, of Dumas, author of histories, novels, significant enough to have a street named after him in the 15th arrondissement. None of his books had ever been translated into English.

Letty was packing, carefully, they only had a week. When the second suitcase was full she asked Paul to zip it. Sitting on it for a moment, she started to talk about another suggestion from family. "I think I probably brought up Père Lachaise and have cemeteries on the mind because of what your brother said last night."

"Andrew is an idiot," Paul said. His brother had called out of the blue to suggest that he and his wife were buying a cemetery plot and wouldn't Paul and Letty like to chip in with them. Not quite out of the blue: Paul and Andrew's parents had both died in the past two years, lung cancer, a stroke—and Paul himself had been in the hospital with an uneven heartbeat, straightened out quickly with medicine, but cautioning. In response Paul grew angry but very quiet, indeed.

It didn't come up again until they were about to land at Charles de Gaulle. Sipping the bitter airplane coffee, Paul surprised Letty, saying, "I don't seem to give a damn where I'm buried. But I've never been very good about death. I closed my eyes to my mother's condition even after she started spitting blood. And there are two or three friends I damned near deserted because I couldn't hack it, not the idea, not the reality."

Letty nodded, sitting on a yawn since the conversation was suddenly so serious. "Let's file it and forget it. In the unlikely event that either of us should turn out to be mortal, we'll think of something."

"Or Sarah and Gabriel will."

And that was an end to the Great Cemetery Plot Problem.

Nothing was said about Père Lachaise for the six days of mostly rain. The last morning was a gift: Paris gleamed, old-new in the rare sunshine. Paul and Letty were both great walkers: spectators at the grand theater of the Paris sidewalks. This morning it was the Isle St. Louis, walking across the Pont des Arts. They held hands as they walked. It was not because they were in Paris, it was because of where they'd been. They'd had a bad patch in their marriage, the accustomed ease of understanding giving way under the pressure of—of what? Paul turning forty, restless, the law not so engaging as it had been before he'd made partner. Letty fired in a sudden downsizing at the private school where she taught, Letty missing the children. Now they were delighted to have come out on the other side, holding hands, walking in Paris, suddenly starving for lunch.

After the second espresso, he looked at her and grinned. She understood perfectly, it was going that way these days. "It's the number sixty-three bus from the Gare de Lyon," Letty said. She'd looked it up that morning, Père Lachaise was too far for a cab and they shouldn't splurge, money was tighter than in the old days. They bought a map at the gate—all the famous names with their path and plot numbers. Letty wanted to see Colette, Paul was interested in Balzac.

Walking up the pretty planted paths, as much like a park as a cemetery, Letty said, "Colette and Balzac, we're like that old Simon and Garfunkel song where she reads her Emily Dickinson and he reads his Robert Frost."

"I remember. 'Dangling Conversation.' Very sad, very Sixties."

They found Colette's grave, modest, subtle, and could not believe that a young woman, actually wearing a hat, was kneeling by the stone monument with a little clump of flowers in her hand. It was all too perfect: the sun slipping between slight puffs of clouds, the easy breeze that hung in the leaves of the plane trees, the girl, clearly moved by her memorial mission.

"We didn't bring anything for Balzac—worse, nothing for the other Paul Gerard." She was silent for a moment as they walked on. "Maybe we *should* get a plot," she said. "So the kids won't be stuck at the last minute."

"Hey," Paul said, adept at avoidance, "here's the great man himself." Balzac towered in Rodin's stone, greatness, ambition incarnate. "Wow," Paul murmured, too impressed even to be silent. Letty, however, was so impressed her natural response was to make a joke; ever the family official jokester. "What a man," she said. "He has delusions of adequacy."

Paul was not amused at humor to topple his hero. He started to move on. Letty caught up and stepped in front of him, surprising him with a kiss, a real one, not a game.

"Don't be embarrassed. This can't be the first time people have kissed in a cemetery."

"If you stay where you are it may be the first time a man has an erection in a cemetery."

"Time will take care of that."

"*Dommage*," he said.

Easy with each other again they idled and got lost along several branching paths. The map was no help and suddenly, around a corner, behind an enormous oak Letty saw the tallest monument thus far. The words Paul Gerard shone, large, in the sunlight, the same sunlight that now dazzled Letty's eyes, made her feel faint, immediately beyond jokes. "Paul Gerard . . ." There was Paul's name carved on the tombstone as they'd always known it was somewhere far away in France and where they'd known it was sure to be someday in America. She swayed, chilled. "Paul," she said. He took it in coolly, the noble scroll-like lettering, the dates 1813-1867, cool enough to be alert when Letty fell against him. He eased her to the ground, a resting nest of leaves, gravel and earth.

She hadn't fainted, was conscious because she said, "It's your—"

Impossibly, shadowing the moment, the sun faded into a fringe of whirling dark clouds. Without sun a chill struck the air. "Hey," Paul said. "Easy does it. Look . . ." He pointed lower down on the obelisk where, in French fashion, a photograph of the deceased was embedded. An irascible, dark middle-aged man, jowly, mordant. Paul was fair, smiles came swiftly to him. "Look," he said. "It's not me. It's him. I told you I'm nowhere near ready."

Letty managed a smile, looked up where the blackness had taken absolute control of the sky. It began to rain lightly at first. Paul pulled her up—ever cautious, even on this perfect day, he had an umbrella but there was no time to open it—and they ran for it. Buses and economy forgotten they hailed a passing cab—unusual in Paris but it was apparently not a usual day. By the time they were safely in, the skies were pouring heavy rain.

"*Americains?*" the cab driver asked.

"*Oui.*"

"I 'ave nevair seen such a change. First warm, *tres doux* . . . then, in one minute freeze, cold and rain. Whoooof."

Paul held a still shaky Letty, warming her. "Sshhh. He turns out to be an awful-looking son-of-a-bitch. Sour. Probably a lousy writer. I'm disowning him. Maybe I'll change my name."

"Seeing your name . . . My God . . . on a tombstone . . . All this time imagining it, kidding around is one thing but this—" She did not look up at him. Breathing deeply as if after a run she said nothing for several long minutes. Then, "Okay, I'm okay now. But— I'm through visiting cemeteries. Except maybe one more time." She tried a smile to see how it would feel. "The only good thing about a cemetery is that when your turn finally comes you're not there."

"You see," Paul said, rocking her a bit in his arms. "There's always a bright side." He gazed down at her huddling in the curve of his arms. "Letty," he said, "one of us has to be good about this stuff. One of us will go first, doesn't usually happen simultaneously."

"Shit," she said, all her recovered good humor gone, for the moment.

"Then don't go," Paul said, taking her role, the temporary jokester to get her through this. Then, as they arrived at their corner, "No, don't open the umbrella in here. It's bad luck."

No need; the sun sang its earlier song. Paris winked at them through a gauze of yellow haze, half wet, half sun, all shimmer and promise. They translated that promise quickly into action. They knew as they fumbled with each other's clothing, the zipper on her skirt, the buttons on his shirt, that they were acting out the convention, passion after cemeteries, love against death. But they were not acting, they were impelled, without thought, and fell in a jumble of arms and legs onto the bed; they had at that moment no desire to be original, only a desire for desire.

Afterwards, sweating in each other's arms Letty murmured, "Second Honeymoon my ass. Just like a couple of kids on their first trip to Paris."

Paul breathed deeply: happy, exhausted. Then Letty was up on one elbow looming, naked, casting a mottled erotic shadow. "Don't the French call all that 'le petit mort'?" She spoke in a little girl's voice. Paul looked up at her, curious. "Only the ecstatic climax. *C'est fort,*" he said, to keep it French, to keep it light.

"Okay," Letty said. "It's all around us this 'mort.' It's fearful foolishness not to go in with your brother."

Paul rose from the damp sheets, sensing a change in the air. "Like buying land—that's all," he said. "Quite small."

Letty tossed him a smile. "Land we have no intention of occupying for about a hundred years."

She grabbed his waist and pulled him back to the tangle of sheets.

"Let's do it!" she said.

"Again?"

"No. Let's call Andrew and tell him okay. Besides," she was able now to rescue a full laugh from the somberness of the occasion. "Besides, we've already seen your place. You've already done it once."

"Right," Paul said, "dying gets easier with practice."

Unembarrassed by nakedness, they threw open the broad casement windows. The Paris sun winked at them through trembling shadows cast by chestnut trees and glinting off the tops of still soaked taxis.

In the distance Notre Dame held its terrifying counsel of faith and mortality.

"It's a shame to leave all this," Letty said, looking at the sudden gift of the fountain in the hotel courtyard and beyond it all the sunny sloping sea of mansard roofs.

"Yes," he said. "It'll be a damned shame."

Je Suis Perdu

Peter Taylor

L'Allegro

The sound of their laughter came to him along the narrow passage that split the apartment in two. It was the laughter of his wife and his little daughter, and he could tell they were laughing at something the baby had done or had tried to say. Shutting off the water in the washbasin, he cracked the door and listened. There was simply no mistaking a certain note in the little girl's giggles. Her naturally deep little voice could never be brought to such a high pitch except by her baby brother's "being funny." And on such a day as this, the day for packing the last suitcases and for setting the furnished apartment in order, the day before the day when they would really pull up stakes in Paris and take the boat train for Cherbourg—on such a day, only the baby could evoke from its mother that resonant, relaxed, almost abandoned kind of laughter.... *They* were in the dining room just sitting down to breakfast. *He* had eaten when he got up with the baby an hour before, and was now in the *salle de bain* preparing to shave.

The *salle de bain*, which was at one end of the long central passage, was the only room in the apartment that always went by its French name. For good reason, too: It lacked the one all-important convenience that an American expects of what he will willingly call a bathroom. It possessed a bathtub and a washbasin, and it had a bidet, which was wonderful for washing the baby in. But the missing convenience was in a closet close by the entrance to the apartment, at the very opposite end of the passage from the *salle de bain*.

Altogether it was a devilish arrangement. But the separation of conveniences was not itself so devilish as the particular location of each. For instance just now, with only a towel wrapped around his middle and with his face already lathered, he hesitated to throw open the door and take part in a long-distance conversation with the rest of the family, because at any moment he expected to hear the maid's key rattling in the old-fashioned lock of the entry door down the passage. Instead, he had to remain inside the *salle de bain* with his hand on the doorknob and his gaze on the blank washbasin mirror (still misted over from the hot bath he had just got out of); had to stand there and be content merely with hearing the sound of merriment in yonder, not able—no matter how hard he strained—to determine the precise cause of it.

At last, he could resist no longer. He pushed the door half open and called out to them, "What is it? What's the baby up to?"

His daughter's voice piped from the dining room, "Come see, Daddy! Come see him!" And in the next instant she had bounced out of the dining room into the passage, and she continued bouncing up and down there as if on a pogo stick. She was a tall little girl for her seven years, and she looked positively lanky in her straight white nightgown and with her yellow hair not yet combed this morning but drawn roughly into a ponytail high on the back of her head.

And then his wife's voice: "It's incredible, honey! You really must come! And quick, before he stops! He's a perfect little monkey!"

But already it was too late. The maid's key rattled noisily in the lock. As he quickly stepped backward into the *salle de bain* and pulled the door to, he called to them in a stage whisper, "Bring me my bathrobe."

Through the door he heard his wife's answer: "You know your bathrobe's packed. You said you wouldn't need it again. Put on your clothes."

His trousers and his shirt and underwear hung on one door hook, beside his pajamas on another. His first impulse was to slip into his clothes and go and see what it was the baby was doing. But on second thought there seemed too many arguments against this,

Je Suis Perdu

His face was already lathered. He much, much preferred shaving as he now was, wearing only his towel. But still more compelling was the argument that it was to be a very special shave this morning. *This morning the mustache was going to go!*

Months back he had made a secret pact with himself to the effect that if the work he came over here to do really finished when the year was up, then the mustache he had begun growing the day he arrived would go the day he left. From the beginning his wife had pretended to loathe it, though he knew she rather favored the idea as long as they were here, and only dreaded, as he did, the prospect of his going home with that brush on his upper lip. But he had not even mentioned the possibility of shaving the mustache. And as he wiped the mist from the mirror and then slipped a fresh blade into his razor he smiled in anticipation of the carrying on there would be over its removal.

In the passage now there was the clacking sound of the maid's footsteps. He could hear her taking all her usual steps—putting away the milk and bread that she had picked up on her way to work, crossing to the cloak closet, and placing her worn suede jacket and her silk scarf on a hanger—just as though this were not her last day on the job; or rather, last day with them in the apartment, because she was coming the following day, faithful and obliging soul, to wax the floors and hang the clean curtains she herself had washed. Their blessed, hard-working Marie. According to his wife, their having had Marie constituted their greatest luck and their greatest luxury this year. He scarcely ever saw her himself, and sometimes he had passed her down on the Boulevard without recognizing her until, belatedly, he realized that it had been her scarf and her jacket, and his baby in the carriage she pushed. But he had gradually assumed his wife's view that their getting hold of Marie had been the real pinnacle of all their good luck about living arrangements. Their apartment was a fourth-floor walkup, overlooking Boulevard Saint-Michel and just two doors from the Rue des Écoles; with its genuine *chauffage central* and its Swedish kitchen, and even a study for him. It was everything they could have wished for. At first they had thought they ought not to afford such an apartment as this one, but because of the children they decided it was worth the price to them. And after his work on the book got off to a good start and he saw that the first draft would almost certainly get finished this year, they decided that it would be a shame not to make the most of the year; that is, not to have some degree of freedom from housekeeping and looking after the children. And so they spoke to the concierge, who recommended Marie to them, saying that she was a mature woman who knew what it was to work but who might have to be forgiven a good deal of ignorance since she had not lived always in Paris. They found nothing to forgive in Marie. Even her haggard appearance his wife had come to speak of as her "ascetic look." Even her reluctance to try to understand a single word of English represented, as did the noisy rattling of the door key, her extreme consideration for their privacy. Every morning at half-past eight, her key rattled in the lock to their door. She was with them all day, sometimes taking the children to the park, always going out to do more marketing, never off her feet, never idle a moment until she had prepared their evening meal and left them, to ride the Metro across Paris again—almost to Saint-Denis—and prepare another evening meal for her own husband and son.

 Yet this maid of theirs was, in his mind, only a symbol of how they had been served this year. It was hard to think of anything that had not worked out in their favor. They had ended by even liking their landlady, who, although she lived but a block away up the Boulevard Saint-Michel, had been no bother to them whatever, and had just yesterday actually returned the full amount of their deposit on the furniture. Their luck had, of course, been phenomenal. After one week in the Hôtel des Saints-Pères, someone there had told them about M. Pavlushkoff, "the honest real-estate agent." They had put their problem in the hands of this splendid White Russian—this amiable, honest, intelligent, efficient man, with his office (to signalize his greatest virtue, his sensibility) in the beautiful Place des Vosges. Once M. Pavlushkoff had found them their apartment they never saw him again, but periodically he would telephone them to inquire if all went well and if he could assist them in any way. And once in a desperate hour—near midnight— they telephoned him, to ask for the name of a doctor. In less than half an hour M. Pavlushkoff had sent dear old Dr. Marceau to them. And Dr. Marceau himself had been another of their angels. The concierge had fetched round another doctor for them the previous afternoon, and he had made the little girl's ailment out to be something very grave and mysterious. He had prescribed some kind of febrifuge and the burning of eucalyptus leaves in her room. But Dr. Marceau immediately diagnosed measles (which they had believed it to be all along, with half her class at L'École Père Castor already out of school with it). Next day, Dr. Marceau had returned to give the baby an injection that made the little fellow's case a light one; and later on he saw them through the children's siege of chicken pox. Both the children were completely charmed by the old Doctor. Even on that first visit, when the little girl had not yet taken possession of the French language, she found the Doctor irresistible. He had bent over her and listened to her heart not through a stethoscope but with only a piece of Kleenex spread out between her bare chest and his big pink ear. As he listened, sticking the top of his bald head directly in her face, he quite unintentionally tickled her nose with the pretty ruffle of white hair that ringed his pate. Instantly the little girl's eyes met her mother's. From her sickbed she burst into giggles and came near to causing her mother to do the same. After that, whenever the Doctor came to see her, or to see her little brother, she would insist upon his listening to her heart. It would be hard to say whether Dr. Marceau was ever aware of why the little girl giggled, but he always said in French that she had the heart of a lioness, and he always stopped and kissed her on the forehead when he was leaving.

That's what the whole year had been like. There was that, and there had been the project—the work on his book, which was about certain Confederate statesmen and agents who, with their families, were in Paris at the end of the Civil War, and who had to decide whether to go home and live under the new regime or remain permanently in Europe.

As far as his research was concerned he had soon found that there was nothing to be got hold of at the Bibliothèque Nationale or anywhere else in Paris that was not available at home. And yet how stimulating to his imagination it was just to walk along the

Rue de l'Université in the late afternoon, or along the Rue de Varenne, or over on the other side of the Seine along the Rue de Rivoli and the Rue Saint-Antoine, hunting out the old addresses of the people he was writing about. And of course how stimulating to his work it was just being in Paris, no matter what his subject. Certain of his cronies back home at the University had accused him of selecting his subject merely as an excuse to come to Paris. . . . He couldn't be sure himself what part that had played in it. But it didn't matter. *He had had the idea, and he had done the work.*

With his face smoothly shaven, and dressed in his clean clothes, he was in such gay spirits that he was tempted to go into the dining room and announce that he was dedicating this book to M. Pavlushkoff, to Dr. Marceau, to Marie, to all his French collaborators.

He found the family in the dining room, still lingering over breakfast, the little girl still in her nightgown, his wife in her nylon housecoat. At sight of his naked upper lip his wife's face lit up. Without rising from her chair, she threw out her arms, saying, "I must have the first kiss! How beautiful you are!"

The little girl burst into laughter again, "Mama" she exclaimed, "don't say that! *Men* aren't beautiful, are they, Daddy?" She still had not noticed that the mustache was gone.

It was only a token kiss he got from his wife. She was afraid that Marie might come in at any moment to take their breakfast dishes. Keeping her eyes on the door to the passage, she began pushing him away almost before their lips met. And so he turned to his daughter, trying to give her a kiss. Still she hadn't grasped what had brought on her parents' foolishness, and she wriggled away from him and out of her chair, laughing and fairly shrieking out, "What's the matter with him, Mama?"

"Just look!" whispered his wife; and at first he thought of course she meant look at him. "Look at the baby, for heaven's sake," she said.

The baby was in his playpen in the corner of the dining room. With his hands clasped on the top of his head and his fat little legs stuck out before him, he was using his heels to turn himself round

Je Suis Perdu

and round, pivoting on his bottom.

"How remarkable!" the baby's daddy now heard himself saying.

"Watch his eyes," said the mother. "Watch how he rolls them."

"Why, he is rolling them! How really remarkable!" He glanced joyfully at his wife.

"That's only the half of it," she said. "In a minute he'll begin going around the other way and rolling his eyes in the other direction."

"It's amazing," he said, speaking very earnestly and staring at the baby. "He already has better coordination than I've ever had or ever hope to have. I've noticed it in other things he's done recently. What a lucky break!"

And presently the baby, having made three complete turns to the right, did begin revolving the other way round and rolling his eyes in the other direction. The two parents and the little girl were laughing together now and exchanging intermittent glances in order to share the moment fully. The most comical aspect of it was the serious expression on the baby's face, particularly at the moment when, facing them and stopping quite still, he shifted the direction of his eye rolling. At this moment the little girl's voice moved up at least one octave. She never showed any natural jealousy of her baby brother, but at such times as this she often seemed to be determined to outdo her parents in their amusement and in their admiration of the baby. Just now she was so convulsed with laughter that she staggered back to her chair and threw herself into it and leaned against the table. As she did so, one of her flailing hands struck her milk glass, which was still half full. The milk poured out over the placemat and then traced little white rivulets over the dark surface of the table.

Both parents pounced upon the child at once: "Honey! Honey! Watch out! Watch what you're doing!"

The little girl crimsoned. Her lips trembled as she said under her breath, "Je regrette."

"If you had drunk your milk this wouldn't have happened," said the mother, dabbing at the milk with a paper napkin.

"Regardless of that," said the father with unusual severity in his voice, "she has no business throwing herself about so and going into such paroxysms over nothing." But he knew, really, that it was not the threshing about that irritated him so much as it was the lapse into French. And it was almost as though his wife understood this and wished to point it out. For, discovering that a few drops of milk had trickled down one table leg and onto the carpet, she turned and herself called out in French to the maid to come and bring a cloth. His own mastery of French speech, he reflected, was the thing that hadn't gone well this year. After all, as he was in the habit of telling himself, he hadn't had the opportunity to converse with Marie a large part of the day, or to attend a primary school where the teacher and the other pupils spoke no English, and he hadn't—with his responsibilities to his work and his family—been able to hang about the cafés like some student. It was a consoling thought. Righteously, he put aside his irritation. But now his little daughter, sitting erect in her chair, repeated aloud: "Je regrette. Je regrette." This time it affected him differently. It was impossible to tell whether she was using the French phrase deliberately or whether she wasn't even aware of doing so. But whether deliberate or not, it had its effect on her father. For a time it caused him to stare at his daughter with the same kind of interest that he had watched his son with a few moments before. And all the while his mind was busily tying the present incident to one that had occurred several weeks before. He had taken the little girl to see an old Charlie Chaplin film one afternoon at a little movie theatre around the corner from them on the Rue des Écoles. They had stayed on after the feature to see the newsreel, and then after the newsreel, along with a fairly large proportion of the audience, they had risen in the dark to make their way out. The ushers at the rear of the theatre were not able to restrain the crowd that was waiting for seats; and so there was the inevitable mélée in the aisles. When finally he came out into the lighted lobby he assumed that his little girl was still sticking close behind him, and he began getting into his mackinaw without even looking back to see that she was there. Yes, it was thoughtless of him, all right; but it was what he had done. As he tugged at the belt of the bulky mackinaw he became aware of a small voice crying out above the noise of the canned music back in the theatre. What in-

Je Suis Perdu

terested him first was merely the fact that he did understand the cry: *"Je suis perdue! Je suis perdue!"* Actually he didn't recognize it as his daughter's voice until rather casually and quite by chance he glanced behind him and saw that she was not there. He threw himself against the crowd that was still emerging from the exit, all the while mumbling apologies to them in his Tennessee French which he was sure they would not understand (though himself understanding perfectly their oaths and expletives) and still hearing from the darkness ahead her repeated cry: *"Je suis perdue!"* When he found her she was standing against the side wall of the theatre, perfectly rigid. Reaching down in the darkness to take her hand he found her hand made into a tight little fist. By the time he got her out into the light of the lobby her hand in his felt quite relaxed. Along the way she had begun to cry a little, but already she was smiling at him through her tears. "I thought I was lost, Daddy," she said to him. He had been so relieved at finding her and at seeing her smiling so soon that he had not even tried to explain how it had happened, much less describe the chilling sensations that had been his at that moment when he realized it was the voice of his own child calling out to him, in French, that she was lost.

Now, in the dining room of their apartment, he was looking into the same flushed little face and suddenly he saw that the eyelashes were wet with tears. He was overcome with shame.

His wife must have discovered the tears at the same moment. He glanced at her and saw that she, too, was now filled with pity for the child and was probably thinking, as he was, that they were all of them keyed up this morning of their last day before starting home.

"Oh, it's all right, sweetie," said his wife, putting her hand on the top of the blond little head and pointing out the milk to Marie. "Accidents will happen."

Squatting down beside his daughter, he said, "Don't you notice anything different?" And he stuck his forefinger across his upper lip.

"Oh, Mama, it's gone!" she squealed. Placing her two little hands on his shoulders, she bent forward and kissed him on the mouth. "Mama, you're right," she exclaimed. "He *is* beautiful!"

After that, the spilt milk and the baby's gyrations were events of ancient history—dismissed and utterly forgotten.

A few minutes later, the little girl and Marie were beside the playpen chattering to the baby in French. His wife had wandered off into the bedroom, where she would dress and then throw herself into a final fury of packing. She had already asked him to make himself scarce this day, to keep out of the way of women's work. His duties, she had said, would begin when it came time to leave for the boat train tomorrow morning. Now he followed her into the bedroom to put on a tie and a jacket before setting out on his day's expedition.

She had taken off her housecoat and was standing in her slip before the big armoire, searching there among the few dresses that hadn't already been packed for something she might wear today. He stopped in front of the mirror above the chest of drawers and began slipping a tie into his collar. He was thinking of just how he would spend his last day. Not, certainly, with any of his acquaintances. He had said goodbye to everyone he wanted to say goodbye to. No, he would enjoy the luxury of being by himself, of buying a paper and reading it over coffee somewhere, of wandering perhaps one more time through the Luxembourg Gardens—the wonderful luxury of walking in Paris on a June day without purpose or direction.

When he had finished with his tie, he discovered that his wife was now watching his face in the mirror. She was smiling, and as their eyes met she said, "I'm glad you shaved it but I shall miss it a little, along with everything else." And before she began pulling her dress over her head she blew him a kiss.

Il Penserosa

The feeling came over him in the Luxembourg Gardens at the very moment he was passing the Medici Grotto at the end of its little lagoon. He simply could not imagine what it was that had been able to depress his spirits so devastatingly on a day that had begun so well. Looking back at the grotto, he wanted to think that his depression had been induced by the ugliness and the triteness of the sculpture about the fountain there, but he knew that the fountain had nothing to do with it. He was so eager to dispel this sudden gloom and return to his earlier mood, however, that he turned to walk back to the spot and see what else might have struck his eye. Above all, it was important for it to be something outside himself that had crushed his fine spirits this way, and that was thus threatening to spoil his day.

He didn't actually return to the spot, but he did linger a moment by the corner of the Palace, beside a flower bed where two workmen—surreptitiously it seemed to him—were sinking little clay pots of already blooming geranium plants into the black soil, trying to make it look as though the plants honestly grew and bloomed there. From here he eyed other strollers along the path and beside the lagoon, hoping to discover in one of them something tragic or pathetic which he might hold responsible for the change he had felt come over him. He would have much preferred finding an object, something not human, to pin it on, but, that failing, he was now willing to settle for any unhappy or unpleasant-looking person—a stranger, of course, someone who had no claim of any kind on him. But every child and its nurse, each shabby student with satchel and notebooks, every old gentleman or old lady waiting for his terrier or her poodle to perform in the center of the footpath appeared relatively happy (in their limited French way, of course, he found himself thinking)—as happy, almost, as he must have appeared not five minutes earlier. He even tried looking farther back on the path toward the gate into the Rue de Vaugirard, but it availed him nothing. Then his thoughts took him beyond the gate, and he remembered the miserable twenty minutes he had just been forced to spend trying to read his paper and enjoy his coffee in the Café Tournon, while a bearded fellow-American explained to him what was wrong with their country and why Americans were "universally unpopular" abroad.

But even this wouldn't do. For he was as used to the ubiquitous bearded American and his café explanations of everything as he was to the ugly Italian grotto; and he disliked them to just the same degree and found them equally incapable of disturbing him in this way. He gave up the search now, and as he strode out into the brightness of the big sunken garden he quietly conceded the truth of the matter: the feeling was not evoked by his surroundings at all but had sprung from something inside himself. Further, it was not worth all this searching; it wasn't important; it would pass soon. Why, as soon as it had run its course with him he would not even remember the feeling again until . . . until it would come upon him again in the same unreasonable way, perhaps in six months, or in a few days, or in a year. When the mood was not on him, he could never believe in it. For instance, while he had been shaving this morning he truly did not know or, rather, he knew not that he was ever in his life subject to such fits of melancholy and gloom. . . . But still the mood was on him now. And actually he understood the source well enough.

It sprang from the same thing his earlier cheerful mood had come from—his own consciousness of how well everything had gone for him this year, and last year, and always, really. It was precisely this, he told himself, that depressed him. At the present moment he could almost wish that he hadn't finished the work on his book. He was able to wish this (or almost wish it) because he knew it was so typical of him to have accomplished just precisely what he had come to accomplish—and so American of him. Generally speaking, he didn't dislike being himself or being American, but to recognize that he was so definitely the man he was, so definitely the combination he was, and that certain experiences and accomplishments were now typical of him was to recognize how he was getting along in the world and how the time was moving by. He was only thirty-eight. But the bad thought was that he was no longer *going to be* this or that. He *was*. It was a matter of *being*. And to *be* meant, or seemed to mean at such a moment, to *be over with*. Yet this, too, was a tiresome, recurrent thought of his—very literary, he considered it, and a platitude.

He went on with his walk. The Jardin du Luxembourg was perfection this morning, with its own special kind of sky and air and its wall of flat-topped chestnuts with their own delicate shade of green foliage, and he tried to feel guilty about his wife's being stuck back there in the apartment, packing their possessions, trying to fit everything that had not gone into the foot lockers and the duffelbag into six small pieces of luggage. But the guiltiness he tried for wouldn't materialize. Instead, he had a nasty little feeling of envy at her packing. And so he had to return to his efforts at delighting in the singular charm of the park on a day like this. "There is nothing else like it in Paris," he said, moving his lips, "which is to say there is nothing else like it in the world." And this pleased him just as long as it took for his lips to form the words.

It wasn't yet midmorning, but the little boys—both the ragged and the absurdly over-dressed-up ones—had already formed their circle about the boat basin in the center, and, balancing themselves on the masonry there, were sending their sailboats out over the bright water. This was almost a cheering sight to him. But not quite. For it was, after all, a regular seasonal feature of the place, like the puppet shows and the potted palm trees, and it was hardly less artificial in its effect.

He was rounding the lower garden of the park now; had passed the steps that lead up toward the Boulevard Saint-Michel entrance and toward that overpowering monster the Panthéon. (There were monsters and monstrous things everywhere he turned now.) He was walking just below the clumsy balustrade of the upper garden; and now, across the boat basin, across the potted flower beds and the potted palms, above the heads of the fun-loving, freedom-loving, stiff-necked, and pallid-faced Parisians, he saw the façade of the old Palace itself. It also loomed large and menacing. There was no look of fun or freedom about it. It did not smile down upon the garden. Rather, out of that pile of ponderous, dirty stone, all speckled with pigeon droppings, twenty-eyes glared at him over the iron fencing, which seemed surely to have been put there to protect the people from the monster—not the monster from the people. It was those vast, terrible, blank windows, like the whitened eyes of a blind horse, that made the building hideous. How could anyone ever have found it a thing of beauty? How could. . . . Then suddenly: "Oh, do stop it!" he said to himself. But he couldn't stop it. Wasn't it from one of those awful windows that the great David, as a prisoner of the Revolution, had painted his only landscape? That unpleasant man David, that future emperor of art, that personification of the final dead end to a long-dying tradition! "Oh, do stop it!" he said again to himself. "Can't you stop it?" But still he couldn't. The Palace *was* a tomb. The park was a formal cemetery. He was where everything was finished and over with. Too much had already happened here, and whatever else might come would be only anticlimactic. And nothing could be so anticlimactic as an American living on the left bank of the Seine and taking a morning walk in the Jardin du Luxembourg. He remembered two novels whose first chapters took for their setting this very spot. Nothing was so deadening to a place as literature! And wasn't it true, after all, that their year in that fourth-floor walkup had been a dismal, lonely one? Regardless of his having got his work done, of his having had his afternoons free to wander not only through the streets where his heroes had once lived but also through the Louvre and the Musée Cluny and through the old crumbling *hôtels* of the Marais? Regardless of the friends they had made and even of the occasional gay evening on the town. Wasn't it really so that he had just not been willing to admit this truth until this moment? Wasn't it so, really, that he had come to Paris too late? That this was a city for the very young and the very rich, and that he, being neither, might as well not have come? What was he but a poor plodding fellow approaching middle age, doing all right, getting along with his work well enough, providing for his family; and the years were moving by.

Suddenly he turned his back on the boat basin and the Palace, and started at a brisk pace up the ramp that leads toward the great gilded south gate. And immediately he saw his daughter in the crowd! She was moving toward him, walking under the trees.

He saw her before she saw him. This gave him time to gather his wits, and to recall that his wife, as soon as she got *him* out of the apartment, was determined to get *them* out, too, so that there would be no one to interfere with her packing. And now, during the moment that she did not see him, he managed to find something that he could be cross with her about. She was ambling along, absentmindedly leaning on the baby's carriage—that *awful* habit of hers—and making it all but impossible for Marie to push the carriage. She had come out from under the trees now, and as she skipped and danced along, her two bouncing blond ponytails, which Marie had fixed, one directly above each ear, were literally dazzling in the sunlight. "Daddy," she said, as she came within his shadow on the gravel path. Her eyes were just exactly the color of the park's own blue heaven. His wife's mother had said it didn't seem quite normal for a girl to have such "positive blue" eyes. And her long little face with the chin just a tiny bit crooked, like his own!

He took her hand, and they went down the ramp toward the row of chairs on their left. "If we sit down, you'll have to pay," she warned him.

"That's all right," he said.

"I'll sit on your lap if you'll give me the ten francs for the extra chair."

"And if I won't?"

"Oh, I'll sit on your lap anyway, since you've shaved that mustache."

The old woman who collected for chairs was hot on their heels. He paid for the single chair and tipped her the price of another.

"I saw how much you gave her," his daughter said reproachfully. "But it's all right. She's one of the nice ones."

"Oh, they're all nice when you get to know them," he said, laughing.

She nodded. "And isn't it a lovely park, Daddy? I think it is."

"It's too bad we're going home so soon, isn't it?" he said.

"Daddy, we just got here!" she protested.

"I mean going back to America, silly," he said.

"I thought you meant to the apartment. . . . But we're not gong back to America *today*."

"No, but tomorrow."

"Well, what difference does *that* make?"

He saw Marie approaching with the carriage. "Let's give our chair to Marie, since I have to be on my way," he said.

"Then you have to leave now?" she asked forlornly.

He gave her a big squeeze with his arms and held her a moment longer on his knee. He was wondering where his dark mood had gone. It was not just gone. He felt it had never been. And why had he lied to himself about this year? It had been a fine year. But still he kept thinking also of how she had interrupted his mood.

And as soon as she was off his knee, he began to feel resentful again of the interruption and of the mysterious power she had over him. He found that he wanted the mood of despondency to return, and he knew it wouldn't for a long while. It was something she had taken from him, something she had taken from him before and would take from him again and again—she and the little fellow in the carriage there, and their mother, too, even before they were born. They would never allow him to have it for days and days at a time, as he once did. He felt he had been cheated. But this was not a mood, it was only a thought. He felt a great loss—except he didn't really feel it, he only thought of it. And he felt, he *knew* that he had after all gotten to Paris too late…after he had already established steady habits of work…after he had acknowledged claims that others had on him…after there were ideas and truths and work and people that he loved better even than himself.

Portrait of a Lady

PAUL THEROUX

A hundred times, Harper had said to himself: *I am in Paris*. At first he had whispered it with excitement, but as the days passed he began mouthing it in a discouraged way, almost in disbelief, in the humiliated tones of woman who realizes that her lover is not ever going to turn up. His doubt of the city made him doubt himself.

He was in Paris waiting for a sum of money in cash to be handed to him. He was expected to carry the bundle back to the States. That was the whole of his job: he was a courier. The age of technology demanded this simple human service, a return to romance: he tucked his business under his arm—the money, the message—as men had a century ago. It was a delicate matter; also, it was illegal.

Harper had been hired for his loyalty and resourcefulness. His employer demanded honesty, but implied that cunning would be required of him. He had impressed his employer because he wasn't hungry and wasn't looking for work. And, a recent graduate of Harvard Business School, Harper was passionate about real estate investment. Afterward he discovered that real estate investment was carrying a flat briefcase with eighty-five thousand dollars in used hundreds from an Iranian in Paris to an office in Boston, to invest in an Arizona supermarket or a chain of hamburger joints. They probably didn't even eat hamburgers, the Iranians—probably against their religion; so much was. Money (he, from Harvard Business School, had to be told this) shows up in a luggage x-ray at an airport security check as innocently as laundry, like so many folded hankies.

I am in Paris. But his first sight of the place gave him the only impression that stayed with him: there were parts of Paris that resembled Harvard Square.

He had told his wife that he would be back the following weekend, and had flown to Paris on Sunday believing that he could pick up the cash on Monday. A day to loaf, then home on Wednesday, and his surprised wife seeing him grinning in the doorway would say, "So soon?"

He had not known that Monday was a holiday; this he spent furiously walking, wishing the day away. On Tuesday, he found Undershaw's office closed—Undershaw was the Iranian's agent, British: everyone got a slice. Harper's briefcase felt ridiculously light. That afternoon he tried the telephone. The line was busy; that made him hopeful. He took a taxi to the office but found it as he had that morning, locked, with no message on the dusty glass. On Wednesday he canceled his flight and tried again. This time there was a secretary in the outer office. She did not know Undershaw's name; she was temporary, she explained. Harper left a message, marked it *Urgent* and returned to his hotel near Les Invalides and waited for the phone to ring. Then he regretted that he had left his number, because it obliged him to stay in his room for the call. There was no call. He tried to ring his wife, but failed; he wondered if the phone was broken. Thursday he wasted on three trips to the office. Each time, the secretary smiled at him and he thought he saw pity in her eyes. He became awkward under her gaze, aware that a certain frenzy showed in his rumpled clothes.

"I will take your briefcase," she said. She was French, a bit buck-toothed and angular, not what he had expected.

Harper handed it over. Not realizing its lightness until it was too late, she juggled it and almost dropped it. Harper wondered whether he had betrayed his errand by disclosing the secret of its emptiness. A man with an empty briefcase must have a shady scheme.

The street door opened and a man entered. Harper guessed this might be Undershaw; but no, the fellow was young and a moment later Harper knew he was American—something about the tortoise-shell frames, the new raincoat, the wide-open face, the way he sat with his feet apart, his shoes and the way he tapped them.

Brisk apology and innocent arrogance inhabited the same body. Still sitting, he spoke to the secretary in French. She replied in English. He gave her his name—it sounded to Harper like "Bumgarner." He turned to Harper and said, "Great city."

Harper guessed that he himself had been appraised. He said, "Very nice."

Bumgarner looked at his watch, did a calculation on his fingers, and said, "I was hoping to get to the Louvre this afternoon."

He is going to say, You can spend a week there and still not see everything.

But Bumgarner said, "What part of the States are you from?"

Harper told him: Boston. It required less explanation than Melrose.

"I'm from Denver," Bumgarner said, and before Harper could praise it, Bumgarner went on, "I'm over here on a poetry grant. National Endowment for the Arts."

"You write poems?" But Harper thought of his taxes, paying for this boy's poems, the glasses, the new raincoat.

Bumgarner smiled. "I've published quite a number. I'll have enough for a collection soon."

The secretary stared at them, seeing them rattling away in their own language. Bumgarner seemed to be addressing her as well as Harper.

"I've been working on a long poem ever since I got here. It was going to be simple, but it's become the history of Europe and in a way kind of autobiographical."

"How long have you been in Paris?"

"Two semesters."

Harper thought: *Doesn't that just sum it up.*

"Are you interested in poetry?" Bumgarner asked.

"I read the usual things at college. Yeats, Pound, Eliot. 'April is the cruellest month.'" Bumgarner appeared to be waiting for him to say something more. Harper said, "There's a lot of naive economic theory in Pound."

"I mean modern poetry."

"Isn't that modern? Pound? Eliot?"

Bumgarner said, "Eliot's kind of a back number."

And Harper was offended. He had liked Eliot and found it a relief from marketing and accountancy courses; even a solace.

"What do you think of Europe?" Bumgarner asked.

"That's a tough one, like, 'Is science good?'" But seeing that Bumgarner looked mocked and wary, Harper added, "I haven't seen much more than my hotel and this office. I can't say."

"Old Europe," said Bumgarner. "James thought it corrupted you—Daisy Miller, Lambert Strether. I've been trying to figure it out. But it does do something to you. The freedom. All the history. The outlook."

Harper said, "I can't imagine any place that has more freedom than the States."

"Ever been to Colorado?"

"No," said Harper. "But I'll bet Europeans go. And for the same reason that characters in Henry James used to come here. To escape, find freedom, live a different life. Listen, this is a pretty stuffy place."

"Depends," Bumgarner said. "I met a French girl. We're living together. That's why I'm here. I mean, I have to see this lawyer. My wife and I have decided to go our separate ways."

"Sorry to hear it." *He will go home,* thought Harper, *and he will regret his folly here.*

"It's not like that. We're going to make a clean break. We'll still be friends. We'll sell the house in Boulder. We don't have any kids."

Harper said, "Is this a lawyer's office?"

"Sure. Are you in the wrong place?"

"Anywhere away from home is the wrong place," said Harper. "I'm in brokerage. I haven't fallen in love yet. As a matter of fact, I'm dying to leave. Is Undershaw your lawyer?"

"I don't know Undershaw. Mine's Haebler—Swiss. Friend of a friend." Then Bumgarner said, "Give Paris a chance."

"Paris is an idea, but not a new one," said Harper. "I tried to call my wife. The phones don't work. Where do these people park? The restaurants cost an arm and a leg. Call this a city?"

Bumgarner laughed in a patronizing way; he didn't argue. It interested Harper to discover that there were still Americans—poets—finding Paris magical. But this poet was getting a free ride:

who was paying? Only businessmen and subsidized students could afford the place. Harper had had a meal at a small restaurant the previous day. The portions were tiny, the waiter was rude, the tables were jammed together, his knees ached from the forced confinement. The meal had cost him forty-seven dollars, with wine. No wonder poets had credit cards. It was a world he understood, but not one that he had expected.

Soon after, a tall man entered: Bumgarner's lawyer. Recognizing him, Bumgarner galloped after him. Harper was annoyed that the poet had shown so little interest in him, and *Eliot's kind of a back number* had stung him. The divorce: he would make it into a poem, deal with it like a specimen in a box and ask to be excused. But the other things—the dead phones, the restaurants, the bathtubs that couldn't take your big end, pillow bolster that was hard as a log, the expense account, the credit card—they couldn't be poems. Too messy; they didn't rhyme. *Go home!* Harper wanted to scream at Bumgarner. *Europe's more boring than Canada!*

The secretary made a sorrowful click of her tongue when Harper rose to go. She had to remind him that he had left his briefcase; empty, it hardly seemed to matter. He was thinking about his wife.

On Friday, Undershaw rang him at ten-thirty, moments before Harper, who had started sleeping late—it was boredom—was preparing to leave his hotel room. Undershaw said he had been out of town, but this was not an apology.

"I've come for the merchandise," said Harper. He wanted to say, *I've wasted a week hanging around for you to appear.*

He said, "I'd like to pick up the bundle today."

"Out of the question."

Harper tried to press him, but gently: the matter was illegal. Undershaw said, "These things take time. I won't be able to do much before next week."

"Monday?"

"I can't be that definite," said Undershaw. "I'll leave a message at your hotel."

No, thought Harper. But he could not protest. He was a courier, no more than that. Undershaw did not owe him any explanation.

Harper had come to the city with one task to perform, and as he had yet to perform it his imagination wouldn't work. He had concentrated his mind on this one thing; thwarted, he could think of nothing else. He was on the hook. His boss had sent him here to hang. Paris seemed very small.

Waiting in Paris reminded Harper of his childhood, which was a jumpy feeling of interminable helplessness. And childhood was another country, too, one governed like this by secretive people who would not explain their schemes to him. He had suspected as a child that there were rules he did not know. In adulthood he learned that there were no particular rules, only arbitrary courtesies. Children were not important, because they had no power and no menace: it took a man twenty-eight years to realize that. You wait; but perhaps it is better, less humiliating, if people don't know you're waiting. Children were ignorant. The strength of adulthood lay in being dignified enough not to expose this impatience. It was worse for women. Now Harper could say to his wife: *I know how you feel.*

The weekend was dreary. Sunday in a Catholic country punished atheists by pushing them into the empty streets. Harper felt unwelcome. He did not know a soul except Bumgarner, who was smug and lucky and probably in bed with his "mistress"—the poet from Colorado would have used that silly word. Harper lay on his bed alone, studying the repetitions in the patterned wallpaper, and it struck him that it is the loneliest traveler who remembers his hotel wallpaper. He was exhausted by inaction; he wanted to go home.

He had been willing to offer the city everything. There were no takers. He thought: All travelers are like aging women, now homely beauties; the strange land flirts, then jilts and makes a fool of the stranger. There is less risk, at home, in making a jackass of yourself: you know the rules there. The answer is to be ladylike about it and maintain your dignity. But he knew as he thought this that he was denying himself the calculated risks that might bring him romance and a memory to carry away. There was no hell like a stranger's Sunday.

* * *

I'll leave a message at your hotel, Undershaw had said. That was a command. So Harper loitered in the hotel on Monday, and when he was assailed by the sense that he was lurking he went out and bought a *Herald-Tribune*; then he felt truant. At five there was no message. He decided to go for a walk, and soon he discovered himself to be walking fast toward Undershaw's office.

"He is not here," the secretary said. She knew before he opened his mouth what Harper wanted.

To cover his embarrassment, Harper said, "I know he wasn't here. I just came to say hello."

The girl smiled. She began to cram papers and envelopes and keys into her handbag.

"I thought you might want a drink," said Harper, surprising himself at his invention.

The girl tilted her head and shrugged: it was neither yes nor no. She picked up her coat and switched off the lights as she walked to the door. Still, Harper was not sure what all this meant, until with resignation she said, "We go."

At the bar—she chose it; he would never have found it in that alley—she told him her name was Claire.

Harper began describing the emptiness he had felt on Sunday, how the only thing it was possible to do was go to church.

Claire said, "I do not go to church."

"At least we've got that in common."

A man in the bar was reading a newspaper; the headline spoke of an election. Harper mentioned this.

Claire thrust forward her lower lip and said, "I am an anarchist." She pronounced the word *anarsheest*.

"Does that mean you don't take sugar?" Harper playfully moved the sugar bowl to one side as she stirred her coffee.

She said, "You have a ring." She tapped it with a pretty finger. "Are you married?"

Harper nodded and made a private vow that he would not deceive his wife.

She said, "How is it possible to be married?"

"I know," Harper said. "You don't know anyone who's happily married. Right? But how many single people are happy?"

"Americans think happiness is so important."

"What do the French think is important?"

"Money. Clothes. Sex. That is why we are always so sad."

"Always?"

"We have no humor," she said, proving it in her solemn tone of voice. "We are—how do you say—*melancholique?*"

And Harper, who knew almost no French, translated the word. Then he complimented her on her English. Claire said that she had lived for two years in London, with an English family.

He wanted her to drink. She said she only drank wine, and that with meals. He took her to a restaurant—again she chose: a narrow noisy room. Why did they all look like ticket offices? Harper stared at the young men and women in the restaurant. The men had close-cropped hair and earrings, the women were white-faced and smoked cigarettes over their food. Harper said, "There's something about this place."

Claire smiled briefly.

"That guy in the corner," Harper said. "He's gay." Claire squinted at Harper. "A pederast."

Claire glanced at the man and made a noise of agreement.

Harper smiled. "A sodomite."

"No," she said. "I am a sodomite. But he is a pederast. *Un pédé.*"

"I knew there was something about this place." Harper's scalp prickled.

"You seem a bit shocked."

"Me?" Harper tried to laugh.

"Didn't you do it at school? Playing with the other boys?"

"They would have killed me. I mean, the teachers. Anyway, I didn't want to. What about you?"

She thrust out her lower lip and said, "Of course."

"And now?"

"Of course."

The food came. They ate in silence. Harper could think of nothing to say. She was an anarchist who had just disclosed that she was also a lesbian. And he? A courier with an empty briefcase, killing time. He thought of the poet Bumgarner: Paris belonged to him. Harper could not imagine the feeling, but Bumgarner would know what to say now.

"It is easier for a woman," said Claire. He guessed that she had perceived his confusion. "I don't care whether I make love to a man or a woman. Though I have a fiance—he is a nice boy. It is the personality that matters. I like clever men and stupid women."

"That guy who was in the office the other day," Harper said. "He's a poet. He writes poems."

Claire said, "I hate poems."

It was the most passionate thing she had said so far, but it killed his ardor.

In the twilight, under a pale watery-blue sky, they walked past biscuity buildings to the river. Although this was his eighth day in Paris, Harper's yearning for home had deserted him, and he could ignore his errand, which seemed trivial to him now. He no longer felt humiliated by suspense; and another thing released him: the girl Claire, who was neither pretty nor ugly, seemed indifferent to him. It did not matter whether he slept with her or not—he felt no desire, so there could be no such thing as failure. He enjoyed this perverse freedom, walking along the left bank of the Seine, on a mild spring evening, feeling no thrill, only a complacent lack of urgency. But that was how it was, in spite of Paris; and urgency had been no help the previous week. He did not speak French. The churches and stonecrusts were familiar; he recognized them from free calendars and jigsaw puzzles and the lids of fancy cookie tins. He had never been overseas before. It was the stage set he had imagined, but he felt unrehearsed.

"I'm tired," he said, to give Claire an excuse to go home.

She shrugged as she had before, but now the gesture irritated him because she did it so well, using her shoulders and hands and sticking out her lower lip.

"I'm staying at a hotel near Les Invalides," he said. "Would you like a drink there?"

She shrugged again. This one meant yes—it was pliable and positive.

By the time they found a taxi rank it was ten-thirty. There was traffic—worse than Boston—and they did not arrive at the hotel until after eleven. The concierge stepped from behind a palm to tell Claire the bar was closed.

Harper said, "We can drink in my room," although he had nothing there to drink.

In the room, Harper filled a tumbler with water from the sink. This he brought to Claire and presented it with a waiter's flourish. She drank it without a word.

He said, "Do you like it?"

"Yes. Very much. It is a pleasant drink."

"Would you like some more?"

"Not now," she said.

He sat beside her on the bed, and kissed her with a clownish sweetness, holding her elbows, and she responded innocently, putting her cool nose against his neck. Then she said, "Wait."

She untied the drawstring at her waist and shook herself out of her dress. She did this quickly, like someone impatient to swim. When she was naked they kissed again, and he was almost alarmed by the way her tongue insisted in his mouth and her foraging hands pulled clumsily at his clothes. Soon after, they made love, and in the darkness, when it had ended, Harper thought he heard her whimper with dissatisfaction.

He woke. She was across the room, speaking French.

"What is it?"

"I am calling a taxi, to go home."

"Don't go," he said. "Besides, I don't think the phone works."

"I have to take my pill."

The phone worked. *I am in Paris*: he said it in a groggy foolish voice.

Claire, who was dressing, said, "Pardon?"

The next day was a repetition of the previous day. He waited at the hotel for Undershaw to ring. At four, he went to the office. This time there were no preliminaries; only romance required them, and this was no romance. Harper was glad of that, and glad too that he was not particularly attracted to Claire. Since his marriage— and he was happy with his wife—he had not been attracted to any other woman. It did not make him calm; indeed, it worried him, because he knew that if he did fall for another woman it would matter and he would have to leave home. They skipped the bar, ate quickly, then hurried to the hotel and went to bed, hardly speaking.

In the pitch dark of early morning, he waited for her to make her telephone call. But she was asleep. He woke her. She was startled then seemed to remember where she was. He said, "Don't you have to go?"

She muttered rapidly in French, then came fully awake and said, "I brought my pill."

Harper slept badly; Claire emitted gentle satisfied snores. In the morning she opened her eyes wide and said, "I had a *cauchemar*."

"Really?" The word, which he knew, bewitched him.

She said, "You have a beautiful word in English for *cauchemar*."

"*Cauchemar* is a beautiful word," he said, and quoted,

How much it means that I say this to you—
Without these friendships—life, what *cauchemar!*

"I don't understand," she said.

"A poem," said Harper.

She pretended to shudder. She said, "What is *cauchemar* in English?"

"Nightmare."

"So beautiful," she said.

"What was your *cauchemar* about?"

"My—nightmare—" she smiled, savoring the word "—it was about us. You and me. We were in a house together, with a cat. It was quite an ordinary cat, but it was very hungry. I wanted to make love with you. That is my trouble, you see. I am too direct. The cat was in our bedroom."

"Where was this bedroom—Europe?"

"Paris," she said. "The cat was so hungry it was sitting on the floor and crying. We couldn't make love until we had fed it. We gave it some food. But when the cat ate the food it caught fire and burned—oh, it was horrible! Each time it swallowed it burned some more. It did not burn like a cat, but like a human, like Jan Palach. You know Jan Palach?"

Harper did not know the name. He said, "A saint?"—because her tone seemed to describe a martyr.

"No, no, no," said Claire. She was troubled.

Harper said, "It's about being a lesbian—your dream. Killing the cat, us making love."

"Of course," she said. "I have thought of that."

Her troubled look had left her; now she was abstracted, her features stilled by thought.

A fear rose in Harper that he was not in Europe at all, but trapped in a strange place with a sad crazy woman. He had made a great mistake in becoming involved with her. It was worse when they were dressing, for the telephone rang and Harper panicked and screamed, "Don't touch it!" He imagined that it was his wife, and he felt guilty and ashamed to be in this room with this incomprehensible woman. He had never loved his wife more. He seized the phone: Undershaw.

"It's ready. You can come over."

"Thank you," said Harper, tongue-tied with gratitude. He turned to Claire. "I've got to go to the office."

But she was buckling her small watch to her wrist. "Look at the time," she cried. "I'm late!"

They arrived separately—it was his idea—so that no one would suspect what they had done. Harper, who had spent days wishing to punch Undershaw in the face, introduced himself to the gray, rather tall Englishman feeling no malice at all. He took the parcel of money and locked himself in a small room to count it. He repeated the procedure, and when he was satisfied the amount was correct he packed the money in neat bunches in the briefcase. And, as if he knew how long it took to count eighty-five thousand dollars, Undershaw knocked at the door just as Harper finished.

"If everything's in order I'll be off then," said Undershaw.

"Take care," said Harper, and watched him go.

In the outer office, Claire was filling her handbag. Harper paused, because he believed it was expected of him to ask her out to dinner—he would not be able to leave until the next day.

Claire said, "I can't see you tonight. I am meeting a woman. I may have an adventure. You can stay—shut the door and it will lock."

"I hope she's nice," said Harper. "Your woman."

"Yes," said Claire, ladylike in concentration. She went to the door and stuck out her lower lip. "She is my fiancé's girl friend."

When she had left, Harper wanted to sit down. But the chairs disgusted him. There were four of them in this dreadful yellow room, this rallying place for the crooked—they were not evil, but idle. The room had held Bumgarner, and Claire, and Undershaw; and now they had gone on their tired errands. But their snailtracks were still here. There are rooms—his hotel room was one—in which the weak leave their sour hope behind; from which they set out to succeed at small deceptions and fail in the hugest way. Harper wanted to be home. He felt insulted and had never hated himself more. The briefcase, weighted with money, reminded him that he was still in Paris, and that he would have to complete his own shameful errand before he could look for a new job in the United States of America.

Rue Guynemer

Lily Tuck

In Paris, she lived on rue Guynemer. Rue Guynemer is named after a very young and very handsome World War I pilot—she knew, she had seen his photograph in the war museum at the Invalides. In the photograph Georges Guynemer is leaning on the fuselage of his biplane; he is wearing a leather helmet with the goggles pushed up against his forehead, and he is looking resolutely away from the camera. According to the caption, the photograph was taken the day before Georges Guynemer was shot down; neither he nor his plane was ever found.

A little oasis, rue Guynemer is a quiet residential street located between Boulevard St. Michel and Boulevard Montparnasse in the heart of the Latin Quarter. The only store on the block is a bookstore, and the apartment buildings, like the one she lived in, are large and comfortable turn-of-the-century Baron Hausmann designs. The main attraction of rue Guynemer lies directly across the street from it: the Luxembourg Gardens. Every day on her way to classes at the Institut Catholique on Boulevard Raspail, she crossed the Luxembourg Gardens and walked by the tethered ponies and donkeys waiting to be hired out for rides, children sailing their boats in the boat basin, young men and women playing tennis, shooting baskets, jogging past her; and always she stopped a moment to watch the same old men playing a game of boules. The routine more than anything else made her feel as if she belonged in Paris and was not just passing through, a foreigner and a tourist. That and her dog—only dogs were forbidden inside the Luxembourg Gardens. The one time she tried, an irate policeman, his navy cape flapping, came rushing over and blew his whistle at her. Couldn't she read the sign? he shouted. The policeman bore an uncanny resemblance to her ex-husband. Or maybe it was his manner.

Her dog, a small, stubborn terrier, was also named George. Only she—the dog was female—was named after a writer, and the sound of the name when she had to make the dog obey: *George! Come here! George, I said, heel!* was harsher and less melodic than the French Georges, spelled with the additional silent and mysterious *s*. *Georges*—she liked to say it the French way, opening her mouth and squeezing the air between her tongue and palate then pursing her lips as if she was getting ready for a kiss.

In Paris, everywhere she went, people were kissing. They kissed early in the morning on their way to buy a baguette, then they kissed some more on their way to work in the Metro; at night it seemed to be worse. She saw people kissing—and not just kissing each other on the lips—in cars waiting for the light to turn green; a lot more people kissed underneath the bridges spanning the Seine, their embraces dramatically lit up by the *bateaux mouches;* they kissed in the movie theaters, blocking her view of the screen; one night as she was walking George, she looked up at a lit window in a building on rue Guynemer and saw two women kissing.

Françoise Sagan, the French novelist—*très riche, très connue*, her concierge informed her—lived here on rue Guynemer.

Ah, oui. *Bonjour Tristesse.*

She had come to France for a change of scene and to learn the language. The fact that she did not know anyone in Paris, she told herself did not matter. The beauty of the city would be enough, she would not be lonely. Strangely enough, there was no specific word for lonely in the French language: *seule, isolée, abandonnée,* she could even use the word *perdue*.

With George pulling at the leash, she took many long solitary walks in her *quartier*, going from rue Bonaparte to St. Sulpice, to Place de l'Odéon, exploring the little streets in between—a lot of the streets were named after French writers: Corneille, Racine, Crébillon, and Regnard—then returning home along rue Vaugirard where Scott and Zelda Fitzgerald had lived for a few months. Their building had large elegant French windows and wrought-iron balconies that opened onto the Luxembourg Gardens; also the setting for the Norths' apartment in *Tender Is the Night:* "high above the green mass of leaves." Each time she went by, it was not hard for her to imagine parties there, and Zelda, in particular, holding a glass of champagne and standing at the window on a warm summer night, looking out with her dark despairing eyes.

Georges Marie Ludovic Jules Guynemer was his full name. A slender young man with the same dark despairing eyes as Zelda Fitzgerald—and it was easy for her to imagine him as well. In fact, she soon had a clearer image of Georges Guynemer than she did of her ex-husband from whom she was separated less than a year. When she thought of her ex-husband—although she tried not to—she found it increasingly difficult to conjure up his face; she could no longer remember whether his eyes were blue or gray. The only feature she could still picture distinctly were his feet. Perfect feet. Jesus feet, she had called them. The kind of feet Michelangelo would have used as a model for his *Pietà*. One time when they were horsing around, her ex-husband, to show off how strong his toes were, pinched her so hard he left an ugly bruise on her arm.

At the Institut Catholique, where she went to learn French, the classrooms were airless and overheated and most of the students, girls working as au pairs, were a decade younger than she was. After class the girls stood in the street wearing their cheap new shoes with thick heels, smoking cigarettes and waiting for boyfriends. The second week, a Russian student whose long hair was tied back with a rubber band and who smelled of onions asked her out for a cup of coffee. They went to a cafe on Boulevard Montparnasse, and the Russian student—he spoke no English—told her in his halting French that he had left his family in Moscow to paint. He asked her to come to his studio which was on the opposite side of the city in the nineteenth arrondissement, and the next evening she took a taxi and did. Yuri's paintings were of ghostlike chairs suspended in brown air and she walked around his studio, which was also his bedroom, looking at the paintings and saying *magnifique* and *merveilleux*. Afterward, since they both could not and did not have anything else to say to each other, Yuri offered her a glass of red wine which she declined, then as if at a loss for what to do next Yuri pushed her down on his bed. For some reason she could not explain—except perhaps Yuri would say she had misled him—she did not resist him. She shut her eyes and let Yuri pull up her skirt and pull down her pants and fuck her. Later, the only thing she remembered clearly about the incident was how Yuri still smelled of onions and how he wore red bikini underpants—a *slip rouge*.

The two long blocks that make up rue Guynemer are intersected by rue de Fleurus and every day except Monday on her way to buy meat she passed number 27 where Gertrude Stein and Alice B. Toklas had lived. (On Monday, traditionally, the butcher shops are shut and only the *chevalines*, the shops that sell horse meat are open and when she first arrived in Paris, she had mistakenly gone to a *chevaline* and bought a pound of purple ground meat. At home realizing what it was, she threw the horse meat directly into the garbage. The horse meat shocked her (she did not even consider feeding it to George.) Monsieur Lacombe, the butcher of the *Boucherie Fleurus,* gave George scraps and took the time to explain to her the different cuts of meat—he had learned a little English, he told her, when at the end of the war American soldiers were stationed in his village in Normandy. As a matter of fact every year, he still received a Christmas card from one of the American soldiers, a soldier named Jack Patterson who lived in California. Did she know California? Did she know anyone there named Jack Patterson? Monsieur Lacombe asked as he chopped, cut, sliced the meat with efficient neat strokes. In the course of this Monsieur Lacombe also told her how his family had been very poor when he was a child and how they only ate meat on special occasions, at Christmas and Easter. Now—and lucky for him—he told her, gesturing with a hand that was missing two fingers, people ate meat every day, people even ate meat twice a day. His wife, Madame Lacombe, sat near the entrance of the *Boucherie Fleurus.* She was the cashier. She frowned when her husband talked too long with the customers; she always referred to him as Monsieur and never by his Christian name, not even when he made a mistake and called out the wrong amount of meat for her to add up.

Monsieur Lacombe retired while she was living on rue Guynemer and his assistant, a young butcher named Jérôme, took over the store. Right away with his pretty blond wife who wore jeans (Madame Lacombe always wore black) and high heels, he made improvements to the *Boucherie Fleurus*. He built shelves and stocked them with expensive canned patès, sauces, spices; he bought a rotisserie on which he grilled chickens, and right away, too, the quality of the meat fell. In addition, Jérôme, overzealous perhaps, cut off a finger on his left hand so that improvements had to come to a temporary halt.

Unfortunately her apartment on rue Guynemer did not look out onto the Luxembourg Gardens but onto a street in the back, rue Madame. *Madame qui?* she was tempted to ask. Rue Madame was so narrow she had the impression that she could reach out from her living room window and touch the apartment directly opposite hers. The windows of that apartment usually stayed curtained and shut, shuttered shut, and only occasionally, on a particularly warm and sunny day, were they opened. Then she was able to look into the interior of the apartment and into rooms that were heavily furnished and old-fashioned and were painted or wallpapered a dull green. She was also able to see the man who lived there. He was a small fat man and something was wrong with him. He would come and stand at the open window and idly wave his hands or else he would jump in place like a rubber ball—bounce, bounce, bounce—one time, she watched as he took down his pants and masturbated.

In addition to not being able to remember what her ex-husband looked like, she could not remember his lovemaking. Instead what stayed in her head was that she seldom came; most of the times with him she had faked it.

She was never quite sure how to pronounce Guynemer; she never knew for certain on which syllable to place the accent: G*uy*nemer or Guy*ne*mer or still yet Guyne*mer*. Whenever she told a French person where she lived or if she took a taxi home, she had to repeat the name at least twice and the driver or whoever she was talking to would invariably say: "Oh, you mean . . ." and repeat the name another way. Each time she thought she finally had it right, someone corrected her.

Georges Guynemer was from the town of Compiègn—at the

American Library on Place de l'Odéon she found several accounts of World War I by American pilots who had joined forces with the elite French *Cigognes* squadron. As a youth, frail in health, Georges Guynemer haunted the airfields and studied the planes and their motors. He was refused by the army several times, eventually he was taken as a mechanic and he learned how to fly. It was not only his intense desire to fight but his coolness in danger that singled him out. It was not unusual for Georges Guynemer to fight six or eight or even ten combats in a single day and to return to his aerodrome with his plane so full of holes it looked like a sieve, his propeller mowed off by bullets. As the war progressed, he became still more unmindful of danger and took greater and greater risks.

For a few weeks after she had gone to bed with Yuri, when they ran in to each other at the Institut Catholique, they continued to smile and say hello but after a while they stopped smiling and after an even shorter while they stopped greeting each other all together. Soon, too, Yuri, she noticed, was arriving and leaving the French classes with his arm around the waist of one of the au pair girls, a tall Danish girl, and she could forget about having gone to bed with Yuri.

At the time when she discovered that her ex-husband was having an affair, an affair with one of her friends, she was both hurt and angry. Also, in a strange way that she did not even try to understand, she had felt relief—relief that she no longer need sleep with him. She and her ex-husband had stayed together another six months before they separated; during that time they continued to sleep in the same bed, and, at night, if accidentally she happened to touch him—her foot hit his calf, her hand brushed his arm—she immediately drew back from him. One time, she woke up to find him caressing her between her legs. Pretending to still be asleep, she let him.

By December the days had grown so short that when she woke up in her bedroom in the apartment on rue Guynemer it was still dark outside at eight o'clock in the morning. She no longer lingered when she crossed the now nearly deserted Luxembourg Gardens—it was always raining or drizzling. Instead, her head bent, she walked quickly looking neither right nor left, the brown leaves from the chestnut trees wet and slippery beneath her feet. *J'aime, tu aimes, il ou elle aime, nous aimons, vous aimez, ils ou elles aimen—*conscientiously, she conjugated verbs in her head—*Je n'aime pas, tu n'aimes pas, il ou elle n'aime—*were it not to signify defeat, she was ready to give up her apartment and return home.

Mid-January, a man named David called her. A mutual friend had given him her telephone number. A lawyer, he was in Paris on a business trip; he hoped she was free for dinner one night that week. "Which night?" she asked him, as if it made a difference. They settled on the next night, he would pick her up at eight. She gave him her address—she had to spell out Guynemer for him—and he joked about how, except for their unpronounceable names, he liked everything about the French, the food, the wine, the women. Especially the women, he repeated with a laugh, and since she did not answer, he asked, "Are you there still?"

"Yes, I'm here," she answered stiffly.

When the doorbell rang the following evening, George ran to the door and barked. The dog's bark was high-pitched and loud. In the living room, she did not move. She was wearing a black silk dress with a low-cut back and she was sitting on the edge of the sofa in such a way as not to wrinkle her dress; also from where she was sitting she could see the front door and she could see George. In between barks, George was sniffing excitedly at the bottom of the door, her stubby little tail wagging back and forth. The bell rang again. Still she did not move. Someone called her name and knocked at the same time on the door. In a frenzy now, George barked louder. The bell rang a third time—a long protracted ring. It rang again and again. Then there was silence. After a while she heard footsteps leaving, going down the stairs. Very deliberately, she got up from the sofa and walked to the front hall. She turned off the lights and went back to her seat on the sofa in the living room. Curious, her tail still wagging, George came over; the dog sniffed her shoes and her legs, up and down.

Georges! she called.

She picked up the dog and the dog, at first, wriggled and squirmed in her lap, then settled down and began to lick her—her hands, her arms, her face.

Although highly decorated and a national hero, Georges Guynemer remained fiercely aloof and did not participate in the good-natured and slightly drunken revels of his squadron mates. About him one of them wrote: "the look on his face was appalling; the glances of his eyes were like blows." Solitary and obsessed with his planes—his last one was a Spad with a 200-horsepower Hispano-Suiza motor; his gun, the latest invention which fired straight ahead through a shaft in the propeller, thus eliminating the need to synchronize the shells between the blades; and, never content or satisfied with how many enemy planes he had shot down—his record was fifty-four, twice as many as Eddie Rickenbacker—Georges Guynemer, she realized, was a virgin.

Two thousand trade paperback copies of
Americans in Paris were printed by Capra Press
in October 2002.
An additional one hundred hardcover copies
have been numbered and signed by
Mr. Gilbar and Ms. Johnson.
Twenty-six copies in slipcases
were also lettered and signed by both.

ABOUT CAPRA PRESS

Capra Press was founded in 1969 by the late Noel Young.
Among its authors have been Henry Miller,
Ross Macdonald, Margaret Millar, Edward Abbey,
Anais Nin, Raymond Carver, Ray Bradbury,
and Lawrence Durrell.
It is in this tradition that we present the new Capra:
literary and mystery fiction, lifestyle and city books.
Contact us. We welcome your comments.

815 De La Vina Street, Santa Barbara, CA 93101
805-892-2722; www.caprapress.com